Treaty Brides

THE CORDIAL BRIDE

SAMANTHA CAYTO

The Cordial Bride
ISBN # 978-1-80250-574-0
©Copyright Samantha Cayto 2023
Cover Art by Kelly Martin ©Copyright October 2023
Interior text design by Claire Siemaszkiewicz
Pride Publishing

Published in 2023 by Pride Publishing, United Kingdom.

Pride Publishing books by Samantha Cayto

Single Books
One Night in a Dungeon
Man Candy
Against a Rising Tide

Alien Slave Masters
The Captain's Pet
The Rebellious Pet
The Untamed Pet
The Captive Pet
The Inconvenient Pet
The Undercover Pet

Alien Blood Wars
Blood Dance
Dangerous Dance
Slave Dance
Star Dance
Mating Dance
Healing Dance
Smoke Dance
Final Dance: Part One
Final Dance: Part Two

Treaty Brides
Boi Bride
The Diplomat's Bride
Stolen Bride
The Substitute Bride
The Secret Bride
The Brigand's Bride
The Cordial Bride

Anthologies
His Rules: Safeword
Right Here, Right Now: Never the Groom

Collections
Rules of Summer: In the Heat of the Dungeon
Dark and Deadly: Dream Demon
S.W.A.L.K.: His True Heart
His Harem: Room for Elijah

THE CORDIAL BRIDE

Chapter One

"When are we going to be there, Mama?"

Ian, Count of Charteris, smiled at his niece's plaintive question. He'd lost track of how many times she'd asked since their journey had begun a few days back. He flashed a smile at his sister. "Yes, when *are* we going to be there, *Mama*?"

Isabeau gave him her usual steely stare. Although she was the younger of them by a couple of years, she had adopted their mother's stern demeanor early in life. She turned her head toward her daughter, for whom she offered a gentler expression. "I believe we crossed the border into Shadow Valley moments ago. It shouldn't be long now until we reach our destination, but if I get that question one more time, Amalie, I shall send you to ride with your nurse."

Amalie rolled her eyes at Ian before saying, "Yes, Mama."

"Good." Isabeau returned her attention to Ian. "And I will take no more nonsense from you, brother. You're the one who volunteered to come on this diplomatic mission. If you're bored already, you have no one to blame but yourself."

"As if I would ever let my widowed sister and niece travel on their own to a foreign land with no treaty in place."

Isabeau pursed her lips. "We're not helpless, Ian, and the king has sent plenty of stout soldiers to protect us."

That was true. They were being accompanied by a few dozen of the king's finest, including two women who nearly dwarfed him in size, to be personal protectors of his sister and niece. He couldn't fault the security, yet there had been no question he would come once he'd heard news of his sister's appointment as special envoy. It was a proud accomplishment for Isabeau, he knew, but it didn't change the fact that the people living in Shadow Valley were unknown to them, and he'd be damned if he went about his merry way while the only two relatives he had left headed into possible danger.

Not wanting to worry his niece in particular, he effected a casual attitude. "Think of this as you doing me a favor, getting me out into the world and broadening my horizons."

Isabeau snorted, an unladylike sound that reminded him she was still the bold girl who'd followed him into all the mischief he'd made in their childhood and not just the staid matron that she'd become since marriage. "As if you've ever wanted to venture beyond the Charteris lands. I thought you'd break out into hives when you came to court to ask the king's permission to accompany me."

Ian didn't bother to correct his sister's impression of how his meeting with the king had gone. 'Asking' was not exactly how he'd characterize what he'd said to the man. There had never been any question as to his coming along. He looked out of the nearest window of the carriage at the rolling valley beyond the thicket of trees lining the road. "This is hardly the same as being in the city. I quite like what I can see so far. Shadow Valley reminds me a bit of home, truth be told."

"It is lovely," his sister agreed. "But I know how much you like getting your hands dirty, and there will be none of that physical labor for you here. As my escort, you will be expected to act as a courtier. Be prepared for the tedium of long meals and mindless chatter."

Ian sighed. "I am." He would hate every minute of the diplomatic dance, but their father had instilled in him his duty to his female relatives. And because he loved these two females more than his own life, escorting them was no hardship.

Isabeau made a noise that indicated how little she believed his reassurance. Then her face lit up. "I suppose it's possible you might finally find your bride here. A marriage would do wonders for a treaty, as well."

Ian didn't bother to sugar-coat his thoughts on *that* topic. "Not going to happen, sister dear. I don't know how many more times I can tell you that I'm *not* going to marry — ever."

"Oh, such nonsense! Really, Ian, you hold a noble title and have a duty to produce an heir."

"I already have one." He winked at Amalie, who listened avidly at their conversation. If nothing else, it broke up the tedium.

Isabeau patted her daughter's hand. "Amalie already has the Truehart estate from her late father. Charteris and the title should go to a child of yours."

This was an old topic of conversation and one that he had little appetite to continue. He stretched his legs as best he could in search of a more comfortable position instead of arguing the point. Carriages were not made for large men. While his sister and niece shared one of the squabs with room to spare, the one he occupied across from them felt like a slightly soft instrument of torture. He would have made the journey on horseback but for his need to stick close to his cherished relatives. If danger made its way past the outriders, he would be the last defense. Gazing at the lushness of the country they entered, it was hard to believe that anything bad happened here. Everything was bright and colorful, with the sun shining down to bathe it all in ethereal light. As a man who reveled in being outdoors, he thought he might find this trip enjoyable after all.

"Mama, I need a break, please." This was Amalie's delicate way of saying she needed to pee.

Truth be told, so did Ian. It would be a nice opportunity to stretch his legs, as well. The journey might be drawing to a close, but he knew their destination to the seat of Shadow Valley's ruling council was a way past the border. He rapped on the roof of the carriage to signal the drivers to stop. A few moments later, they did. Ian waited until the lead soldier shouted orders for his men to fan out to keep watch before opening the carriage door. He stepped out first, nearly groaning with relief, before handing his sister down. She stood to one side, shaking out her voluminous skirt as he lifted Amalie by her waist to set her beside her mother. The child was ten now, and it was disconcerting to notice how much she was heading into womanhood already. She bobbed a curtsy in thanks before her nurse came up from the carriage behind them to take her by the hand. His sister's maid was close on the woman's heels to serve her mistress' needs.

Ian scanned the area for any sign of danger before saying, "I'll be nearby if you need me."

Isabeau waved him off before turning to join Amalie and the other women. Ian walked in the opposite direction to find a private spot to relieve himself. Beyond a stand of trees, he came upon a lovely lake with crystal-clear blue water and a small outcrop of rocks across the way. He took a deep breath of the clean, sweet-smelling air as he undid his laces to release his dick and turned his face into the heat of the sun. Shadow Valley was poorly named if this bit of it was representative of the whole country. A movement by the rocks caught his attention. He had his sword out of its scabbard in an instant. In the next one, he relaxed as someone came into view. No, not someone, a vision of beauty that overtook the landscape around them.

Ian had grown up on tales of woodland folk— fairies…beautiful creatures who flitted about the natural part of the world that they called home. For one wild moment, he thought they had been more than mere stories, that such otherworldly beings really did exist. It was a fanciful thought but not surprising, given the pale, slender boy with long, golden hair standing gloriously naked on top of the rocks. Even at a distance, his beauty was arresting, and he might have been mistaken for a girl if not for his obvious maleness on display. With amazing grace, the boy lifted his arms and dove into the water.

Ian followed the arc of movement with his gaze, then moved for a closer look when the boy didn't immediately come back up. Something bright flashed under the water before breaking through to the surface with a splash. As Ian stood by the bank, staring like a fool, the pretty boy shook his head and dragged his wet hair away from his face with his fingers. He treaded water and grinned at Ian. His gaze flicked downward, and his grin grew wider.

It took Ian a moment to realize he'd forgotten to resheath his sword and do up his laces. In its unconfined state, his dick had no trouble standing, hard and eager, signaling the instant desire he had felt at the first sight of this water nymph. He carefully put away his sword so that he didn't accidentally castrate himself. But when he grabbed his cock to stuff it back into his trousers, the boy gave a cheeky wave before diving back under. The sight of a slick, small rump hovering above the surface before submerging had Ian coming with a surprised grunt. He'd been careful not to tend to this need during the journey out of respect for his sister. His dick had been unable to behave itself in the face of such bold temptation, however. His seed spilled on the ground, leaving him nearly dizzy with the force of it.

He stood staring long after the tremors of his climax had subsided and his dick softened enough to be confined back behind his laces where it belonged. Like some sappy young man, he longed for another glimpse of the boy. It wasn't until he heard his sister's voice calling to him and cutting through the fog of desire that he pulled himself together and headed back to the road.

Still, he couldn't resist a glance over his shoulder. There was nothing to see except the nature around him. It was almost as if he'd imagined the whole encounter.

Except he hadn't.

* * * *

Calan raced home, letting the wind dry his hair as his horse galloped across the fields. It had been naughty of him to indulge in his whim for a ride and a swim in the lake. His aunt had stressed repeatedly that he had to be ready to greet the strangers who were expected any time now. As a member of the ruling council, she had to be part of the welcoming party, and as her only relative, he was required to hover in the background in support of her. All the rules of etiquette bored him silly. He much preferred being out and about, exploring their land and working in the garden. That was where his true talent lay. Stuffing him into his best clothes and forcing him to socialize was torturous for him and of no value to his people. A possible treaty with the mighty Moorcondia was important to Shadow Valley, to be sure, but no one should be counting on *him* to help with that endeavor. He had no diplomatic skills and was terrible at making small talk.

As he arrived at the stables, however, his mind wandered back to what had happened by the lake. He had very likely been the first of his people to make an impression on one of their guests. And although he was inexperienced in the ways of sex, he knew enough to understand he'd made a very *good* impression on the man, at least. Just the thought of the large, hard cock waving at him sent his own dick and balls tingling. He forced a stop to his burgeoning arousal. There was no time for that nonsense. He contented himself with the knowledge that he would soon see the man again up close. There was no way he was merely a soldier, not given his mode of dress. Because Calan knew the Moorcondian envoy was a woman, he wondered who the man was. *Her husband, no doubt.* A pity. It would have been nice to at least flirt with such a handsome and powerful-looking man. It would have been nicer still if Calan had finally found a man who could deflower him without the sticky complications of seeing each other every day under his aunt's watchful eye.

There was no more time to dwell on it. His aunt called out his name in the tone of voice that warned him he was on the wrong side of her temper already. Calan handed his horse off to a stable boy, who gave him a sympathetic look before heading for the barn. Knowing that any further delay would be to his detriment, Calan ran to the back door of the cottage he shared with his only living relative. Aunt Celia had raised him since his parents' death, and he really owed her respect and gratitude. He just wished she'd loosen up a little. Sometimes he worried that she'd crumble to tiny bits if her hard façade was cracked even a small amount. She was implacable on everything and was not happy at the prospect of forming a treaty with any country. Everyone knew that she'd opposed the vote to accept Moorcondia's overture, vociferously so. But she also did her duty, no matter her personal feelings. His tardiness couldn't be helping what had to be already-fraught nerves.

He raced to where she stood, tapping her toes. "Sorry, Aunt. I lost track of time. I won't be more than another moment." He slipped past her to enter the cottage, feeling the lash of her tongue, despite her silence.

It didn't take long for him to make himself presentable. His swim in the lake had left him clean and refreshed, and he didn't have many clothes. He donned his good tunic and trousers in light blue that he was vain enough to think set off the color of his eyes to good effect and belted it with the leather braid he'd made himself. His formal brown boots were already polished to as glossy a shine as he could manage, so all that was left to do was fix his hair. He braided it into a tail that hung over his shoulder as he hurried back down to his waiting aunt. With a quick grin, he stood for inspection.

Aunt Celia gave a curt nod. "You'll do." Her own attire was its usual simple black gown with only a green beaded belt to give it any color. She wore her hair in such a severe bun that her face always looked as if it might split in two if she twitched a smile—which she rarely did and never for long. "Come along. The sentries have already sounded the alarm. Our *guests* are about to arrive."

Calan followed a half-step behind her, always the dutiful nephew in public. It didn't take long to arrive at the longhouse. Celia's high station meant she had a house near to the square that served as the hub of their people. A large crowd had already gathered, not surprising given the historic nature of the envoy's arrival. Shadow Valley wasn't exactly cut off from the rest of the world, but other than traders, they rarely saw people from neighboring lands. The prospect of doing a formal treaty with a country as powerful as Moorcondia was exciting—and frightening. His aunt and others who thought like she did warned that they would be overtaken if they didn't watch their step.

Moorcondia might say they were looking for a treaty, but they could be scouting out a possible means of attack. Calan couldn't see the logic in that thinking. If the man he'd seen was any indication, the Moorcondians looked to be powerful enough to conquer them without subterfuge.

They joined the rest of the council and their families by the entrance to the longhouse. Everyone was dressed in their finest clothes and every pair of eyes was trained on the direction their guests were arriving from. The sound of horse hooves heralded the Moorcondians' approach. Then a line of large soldiers came into view. There was a collective gasp and some murmurs at the sight. It was impressive and scary. Although none of the men had weapons drawn or were doing anything menacing, it was obvious how that could change in a moment. But then a beautiful carriage followed, and now the reaction of his people was more like awe. That conveyance was large and covered in colorful heraldic signs and gilded edges. If nothing else, these strangers were displaying their wealth. More men and another, less-elaborate carriage followed. At least a dozen additional soldiers brought up the rear. The entire procession pulled up in front of the longhouse. Now the crowd had gone silent as everyone watched and waited for what was to come next.

A soldier dismounted and opened the door of the first carriage. Calan was probably the only one who wasn't surprised to see a large man emerge from the conveyance. Up close, he was even more impressive than he'd been by the lake. He was easily a head taller than the average Shadow Valley man, which Calan couldn't count himself among. He would barely reach the top of this man's chest, not that such a measurement would ever be made, he quickly reminded himself. The Moorcondian was the epitome of masculine beauty, with a square jaw, long, straight nose and high cheek bones. His light-brown hair was styled in a casual mess of waves that skimmed his shoulders. Like Aunt Celia, he was dressed entirely in black, but these clothes had style, with golden embroidery along the collar, cuffs and hem, and his knee-high black boots shined more brightly than Calan could ever achieve with his own. And there was a sword belted at his waist—something Calan had barely noticed by the lake, distracted as he'd been by the man's cock—but the weapon was also obviously not merely for decoration. This was a soldier as well as an aristocrat. That much was obvious.

The Moorcondian man stood for a second, scanning the crowd, His gaze skimmed over Calan, then returned quickly to bore a hole into him. Calan's cheeks heated under the scrutiny of dark eyes, and when the man smiled oh so briefly, a strange warmth settled in Calan's groin. It was a relief when the man turned his attention back to the carriage. He offered his hand to someone inside, and a woman alighted a moment later. This was the envoy, and she was every bit as interesting, although Calan wasn't attracted to women. Unlike everyone else so far, she was dressed in bright colors of yellow and gold. Her gown had a full skirt the likes of which Calan had never seen before. Obviously, she did no physical labor. She had the same look about her as the man, except her hair was mostly covered by an elaborate type of kerchief that had a bejeweled band above her brow.

The woman smiled brightly as she headed toward the leader of the council. There was nothing in particular that caused Fennic to stand out as such, yet this diplomat obviously had a trained eye. She curtsied in front of him. "My lord, Fennic, thank you for greeting me."

Momentarily flustered, Fennic flicked his gaze around before giving a shallow bow. "Lady Isabeau, it is my great pleasure. And please, call me Councillor. We have no lords or ladies here, only elected members of our governing body. It is my humble duty to hold the headship for a few more years yet."

Lady Isabeau's smile didn't waver. "Of course, Councillor. Your manner of government is one of the many intriguing aspects of your country that I hope to get to know better."

Pretty words, but everyone knew that Moorcondia wasn't there for lessons in politics. It was rumors of Shadow Valley's most recent cordial that had precipitated this overture. The people of the Valley had the best medicines, given their lands' diverse flora. Everyone knew that. But this latest concoction had the power to change people's lives by avoiding terrible death. Calan was all for sharing in the marvel, but it wasn't his decision to make, and the idea of the upcoming dance of negotiation he was sure would take place intimidated him. He had no skill at such things, nor was he interested in the ensuing introduction of the rest of the council, so he trained his focus on the man he assumed was the envoy's husband.

Fortunately, the Moorcondian wasn't looking at him. He'd turned his attention back to the carriage and lifted out of it a girl who was obviously the envoy's daughter. She was the spitting image of the woman, except her violet-colored gown was simpler and her hair was uncovered. It was tamed in complex braids wound with silver ribbon. She was like a bright and beautiful creature among the more plainly dressed girls clinging to their mother's skirts as they watched the proceedings. Taking her by the hand, her father led her over to her mother.

Lady Isabeau gestured toward them. "May I introduce my daughter, Mistress Amalie Charteris Truehart of Truehart Manor." When the girl curtsied with the same grace as her mother had, the woman continued. "And this is my brother, Ian, Count of Charteris. He was keen to see your lovely country for himself, and our king kindly gave him permission to accompany me."

A weird sort of relief rushed through Calan. *Brother, not husband.* Now when the man glanced in his direction, Calan permitted himself to smile back at him. He had little experience with flirting but hoped the man would understand that was what he was doing. The heated gaze he got in return told him he did.

The man sketched a bow to the council. "I hope my presence is acceptable to you. Since my sister is widowed, I thought it appropriate to escort her. Although as she implied," he added with another flick of his eyes in Calan's direction, "I am keen to explore the beauty of your land."

Fennic waved with open arms. "Of course, Count. You are most welcome, and no man here can fault your admirable concern for your sister's welfare. I assure you, however, that she and her lovely daughter are quite safe with us."

"Of course," the count agreed with an affable tone that nevertheless conveyed that his guard was not down.

Celia stepped forward. "If you care to enter our longhouse, Lady Isabeau, we have refreshments for you and your…entourage to partake in before we begin our discussions."

"How very kind. Thank you. And I look forward to discussing the many ways a treaty with Moorcondia can benefit both your people and ours."

Being a diplomat, she was careful not to mention the cordial, but everyone knew the rumors had spread about it and that was what had brought the woman here after many generations of their people knowing about each other.

Fennic nodded. "Indeed, we are also looking forward to it. This way, if you please." He led them through the doors.

The family members of the twelve councilors filed in behind them, leaving the rest of their people to go about their business. Normally, Calan hated these command performances of social interaction. This time, he was eager to be a part of things. It gave him a chance to get a better look at the count, although he was seated at the far end of the long communal table, and it was hard to do any more than glance at the man across the expanse of food between their two sides. And it might have been his imagination, but he could swear that the man was perusing him, as well. Every time Calan dared to look at him, he was staring back. Toward the end of the meal, the count even winked at him. Calan was wide-eyed with shock at the brazen flirtation and must have turned beet red, given how hot he felt. He realized he was out of his depth with a man like the count, so he kept his head down until everyone rose from the table.

Lady Isabeau said, "A delicious meal, Councillor Fennic. Thank you."

"You are most welcome. Shall we retire to the council room to begin our discussions?" Fennic gestured toward the door at the far end of the longhouse.

Only council members and those serving them refreshments ever entered it, but Calan knew, as everyone did, that it held a great round table to demonstrate that all the council members had equal power.

As curious as he was about the Moorcondian, Calan wanted the freedom that came from leaving. He needed time to get used to these new feelings of mutual attraction and was always happiest when wandering alone in nature. Before they were all dismissed, however, Lady Isabeau made a request.

"I wonder if it's possible for someone to show my daughter and brother some of your charming town? The journey was long, and a good walk would be appreciated."

"Of course." Fennic looked around for someone suitable.

Before he could ask anyone to perform that duty, the count interjected. "How about this young man?" He pointed at Calan. All heads turned in his direction, and he froze with the scrutiny.

Aunt Celia frowned. "That is my nephew, Calan. He is not part of the government and merely helps me with my work as an apothecary and healer."

"Indeed?" The count smiled ingratiatingly. "Then he sounds like the perfect person to introduce me to your flora. I work my lands myself and have a keen interest in farming. With your permission of course, madam."

Aunt Celia was clearly not pleased with the idea, probably worried that Calan would give away the secret of their new cordial before the treaty was negotiated. She saw him as obtuse at the best of times, more interested in plants than people, and he didn't mind cultivating—so to speak—that perception. He would never do such a thing, of course, unless he knew it was what the council wanted. The protection of Shadow Valley was every bit as important to him as it was to everyone else. Spending time close up and mostly privately with the man so soon after meeting him was a daunting idea, too, the complete opposite of what he'd just resolved to do. If he didn't take advantage of the forced opportunity, however, his virginal state might last forever.

He dared to step forward. "I would be delighted to, Aunt." He gave them all his best vacant expression, as if he had no more thoughts in his head than a butterfly.

Fennic intervened before Aunt Celia could respond. "An excellent suggestion."

The count held out his hand to his niece. "Marvelous. Come, Amalie."

The girl didn't hesitate to clasp hands with her uncle. Her nurse kept one step behind her. "What shall we see first?" she asked Calan. She was a far more self-assured child than he'd ever been.

The answer was easy, though. "The decorative gardens. They don't serve a useful purpose other than enjoyment, but I'm sure you'll like what there is to see." Calan let his gaze encompass the count.

The man's heated look back was unnerving. "I already do."

Chapter Two

Ian tried to be polite and look at all the local sights his adorable guide was pointing out, but truth be told, nothing compared to the boy's beauty and allure. His gaze kept wandering back to him, which made Calan charmingly blush — or at least Ian believed he was the cause of the pink stain across those lovely cheeks.

For someone who apparently spent a lot of time outdoors, the Shadow Valley boy was surprisingly pale. Seeing him up close did nothing to dispel his first impression that he was seeing a woodland sprite, either. There was something ethereal about Calan that stood in stark contrast to the rugged and plain people of this place. That was especially true of the boy's aunt. *What a dragon.* The woman's displeasure at their arrival had been palpable. Ian had resolved on the spot to keep an eye on her, and what better way to do that than spend time with her kinsman?

Oh, well done, the perfect rationalization for giving in to my temptation.

Calan was doing nothing to dissuade him from his interest, either. The boy was flirting with him, and his obvious lack of experience made his efforts delightfully entertaining. He hoped his hosts had nothing against men pleasuring each other, because Ian intended to accept the invitation thrown his way at the first opportunity. Of course, nothing would happen so long as Amalie and her nurse were with them, but the waiting would make the attainment that much more satisfying.

With a sudden squeal, his niece tugged at his hand. "Look, Uncle Ian!"

Ian forced his gaze to switch to where his niece was pointing. They had come upon animal statues made entirely of bushes. "How marvelous." He glanced at Calan. "I thought my king was the only one to have a topiary."

The color on the boy's cheeks intensified. "Really? I didn't know anyone else carved animal shapes out of shrubs until I came across the idea in an old book a few years ago. I thought perhaps it was a practice that might have died out and that I was happy to revive. It's great fun to do."

Ian let his surprise show. "You did all this?" As they came upon the first figure—a miniature horse—he let go of Amalie's hand so that she could get a closer look, then turned to face the boy.

Calan stopped as well, fidgeting with his fingers, and lowering his gaze. "Yes. No one else really has time to do it. We are a farming community, after all, and the days are long."

Ian's own fingers itched with the desire to touch a few strands of blond hair that had escaped their braid. He clasped his hands behind his back to quell the temptation. "As someone who works his land, I well know how much time and effort goes into growing food and managing stock. Do you not labor in that way?" He knew the answer already. No one with such soft-looking skin and lithe body tilled the soil or looked after flocks.

Calan's eyelashes fluttered and he quirked his lips up in a quick grin. "No. I help my aunt with her potions, mostly by gathering what she needs and tending to the sick. It doesn't take much time, and as our family has always acted as apothecaries and healers for our people, we don't have a farm."

It occurred to Ian that here might be a source of information about the cordial his sister sought to secure for Moorcondia, but he put it aside immediately. He was not the diplomat for this visit. Isabeau knew what she was about, and his only job was to make sure she and Amalie were safe. Other than perhaps seducing Calan, he had no tasks to accomplish while visiting Shadow Valley. Another squeal from his niece caught his attention before he could ask more personal questions of their guide.

"Uncle Ian, you must come and see this rabbit!"

With a quick smile at Calan, he wandered over to where she stood. Up close, he could see the detail put into the figures. "Wonderful." He turned to Calan, who had come up beside him. "You have a marvelous talent."

The boy's blush deepened even more, if that were possible. "It's not that hard, actually."

Now Ian did give into temptation. He slowly brought up his hand to pluck the wayward strands and tuck them behind the shell of one of Calan's pretty ears. A visible shiver ran through the boy, and he peeked at

Ian from under his lashes. Ian's cock, already in a semi-state of arousal, went rock hard. If they'd been alone, he'd have pulled the fetching boy into his arms for a kiss—perhaps more. But Amalie was dancing around them, and her nurse had half an eye on her charge and half on Ian—his sister's spy, no doubt. So, dropping his hand, he went back to clasping it behind his back and wandered through the topiaries.

When they came upon a large, flowering hedgerow with an arched opening, Amalie squealed yet again and raced toward it. Ian winced at her unladylike demeanor. Although he didn't mind, he figured his sister might have something to say to Amalie about it later. The girl had promised to be on her best behavior when she'd begged to come along. The nurse's indulgent smile, however, relieved him. The woman adored Amalie and probably wasn't going to tell any tales. He certainly wasn't.

As he and Calan approached the opening, the boy said, "It's a maze, Mistress Truehart. If you venture in, there's a marvelous surprise waiting for you in the center."

With wide-eyed excitement written on her face, Amalie looked at Ian. "May I, Uncle?"

"Of course. If you get lost, I'm sure we can find some bloodhounds to sniff you out." He grinned broadly.

Amalie giggled and disappeared into the maze, her nurse hurrying to keep up. Ian strolled over to the hedgerow and plucked one of the pink flowers among the greenery. He twirled it in his fingers for a few seconds before sticking the stem through Calan's braid at a point by his ear. "Ah, the perfect complement to your creamy complexion. I hope you don't mind my boldness."

Calan gnawed at his lower lip before staring Ian in the eyes. "I've been counting on it, actually. You're unlike any man I've ever met."

The smile Ian gave him was slow and provocative. "And you are the most beautiful boy I've ever seen."

Calan's cheeks went from pink to deep red, and he looked away. "That is kind of you to say."

"Kindness has nothing to do with it, my dear." Sensing that he was moving too fast for this undoubtedly innocent boy, he entered the maze and was impressed with the complexity of it. The sound of Amalie's giggles had him turning left. "She won't actually get lost in here, will she?"

Now it was Calan who giggled, a sound that danced along Ian's nerves in a way that his niece's never did. "No. The maze is big but not tricky. It's one of the few ways my people indulge themselves, as it serves no useful purpose." The boy undoubtedly knew his way around the place, yet he kept a half-step behind Ian, letting him lead the way. "May I ask you something, my lord?"

"Of course…and call me Ian."

"Thank you. That seems too familiar, though. My aunt would disapprove."

Ian made a show of looking around. "I don't see her here at the moment."

"You are far bolder than I."

Ian sighed. "The product of my being a count, I suppose."

"That was what I wanted to ask you about. How did you become a count? I'm sorry if that's rude. It's only that we don't have such things in Shadow Valley."

"Ah yes, your ruling council is chosen by the people." It was an intriguing idea to allow the populace to pick their leaders, one that he doubted would catch on in his own country.

"All citizens sixteen and older vote every ten years on who sits on the council. And if we don't like what they're doing, we can vote them off again. I've only had the chance to choose once since I passed into adulthood, and to be honest, it's usually the same people serving, anyway. It's a lot of work, although someone like my aunt thrives on the power. Not that she's a tyrant or anything," he added hastily.

"Of course not," Ian readily agreed, although if anyone had the capacity for the thirst of control over others, he sensed that she would.

"Anyway, I assume you weren't elected to be a count."

Ian chuckled at the idea. "No. I was born into it. One of my long-ago ancestors helped the first king of Moorcondia solidify his power and was rewarded with the title and the lands that make up Charteris. I was fortunate enough to be born the oldest, so it's mine now that my father is dead."

"And a child of yours will inherit the title when you are gone?"

Ian shook his head. "No. I have no wife or children. Amalie will one eventual day be the Countess of Charteris. If I die before my sister, she will inherit the title, and after her comes her daughter."

"But you could have children of your own someday. I mean you are far from an old man. Surely you'll marry at some point."

"I won't become a father because I will never marry." Ian stopped to stare at Calan full on. He gave him an appraising look. "Women don't interest me as bed partners. I prefer a masculine form." He let his gaze

to be off limits. She wanted to keep him all to herself in furtherance of her work. Attention by another would distract him from her needs, and while her possessiveness had never really bothered him before, the confinement was starting to chafe. The count would be different, however, being independent of her influence and having the added value of being temporary. Whatever happened between them, the man would soon be gone, never to be seen again, in all likelihood. The idea of it, to his surprise, saddened him. He barely knew the man. It was silly to mourn his loss before he'd even experienced being with the man in any intimate way.

"Come on. We mustn't keep our *guests* waiting." Aunt Celia didn't wait to see if he was following as she walked out of the door, certain of his obedience. "The cheek of the woman," she declared in a low voice while they hurried to the longhouse. "She's so sure she'll get her hands on my potion. You can see it in her expression, no matter the honeyed words she uses to cajole the council."

"She wants to benefit her people, Aunt." The withering glance his aunt gave him made him wince.

"We all want to help our own, but where will we be if we give away too much of the precious cordial?"

Calan didn't bother to point out that the ingredients were plentiful and probably found all over Moorcondia and not only in Shadow Valley. The gain of one country didn't mean a loss to the other. His aunt was in high dudgeon over the matter, and no amount of logic was going to change her attitude. "I'm sure the meeting was difficult. Fennic and many of the other council members are keen on opening up more trade with Moorcondia. It's probably all they can think of." He agreed with their position yet was not so foolish as to say so. His aunt needed to get out some of her *mad* before the evening meal, and he was the safest place for her to do it.

"Huh! That is too right. Fools, all of them." She was quiet for a moment before changing the direction of the conversation in a more uncomfortable way. "And the nerve of that brother of hers, demanding that you waste your time entertaining him. He didn't do anything offensive, did he?" She punctuated her question by grabbing his arm and turning to stare hard into his eyes.

Calan did his best to look innocent, even as his cheeks felt hot. "No, ma'am. He was very formal and proper. I, um, showed him and his niece the maze. That kept them occupied for most of the time."

Aunt Celia harrumphed before letting him go. "Then that should be end of it. He has no business here, and I won't have him insisting that you entertain him by showing him the sights. Or worse," she added with particular bitterness. "I don't like the way he looked at you."

"Please don't worry, Aunt Celia. I can handle myself…and him." As statements went, it was true, just not entirely honest. He was fairly confident that the count wouldn't pressure him into anything he wasn't comfortable with. The man appeared to be the epitome of a nobleman—honorable and confident enough not to be brutal. If his niece was anything to go by, the man was kind and trustworthy, as well.

"He better not try anything with you," she continued as if he hadn't spoken. It was hard not to feel insubstantial around her. "If he does, I'll give him something to make his manhood shrivel."

With a wince, Calan was quick to reassure her. "He won't. If nothing else, he seems devoted to his sister and wouldn't want to hurt her mission here."

That observation only served to increase her ire. "Ha! Controlling, more like. As if he has anything of value to add to her efforts. Foppish man. He probably sits around, never putting in an honest day's work. Soft and vane."

Calan knew when it was time to keep his mouth shut. None of those descriptions fit the man he'd spent so much time with already. Ian was a strong man who obviously spent a lot of time doing strenuous activities, and as for soft...? The man's hand had been calloused in the way of a laborer. When he'd done the extraordinary thing of putting a flower in Calan's braid, the rough skin of his thumb had brushed Calan's earlobe. Just thinking of the moment sent a delightful shiver down his back.

They were among the last to enter the longhouse. Calan's couldn't help looking for Ian the moment he stepped into the large room. The man was easy to spot, towering over everyone. He was dressed very finely indeed, his black tunic and trousers embroidered with silver thread throughout, and his high boots gleaming like mirrors. Calan wondered if the man ever wore any other color. The count was focused on his sister, who was speaking with Fennic, then his gaze shifted abruptly toward Calan before he'd taken more than two steps into the room. The intensity in the man's eyes was unnerving, and the way his lips curved up into an inviting smile made Calan grateful that he'd chosen to wear small clothes for the evening. The extra layer hid his reaction to such scrutiny.

Calan dared a quick grin back before dutifully following his aunt as she joined the group surrounding Lady Isabeau. Amalie was nowhere to be seen, apparently deemed too young to join the formal evening meal. It was something of a relief and a worry that the little girl wasn't going to act as a natural restraint on his interactions with the count. *No, Aunt Celia will fill that role well enough.* It was bold and perhaps silly to even expect to have some kind of personal interaction with their visitor on such short acquaintance, but Calan felt more than ready to fully enter the world of adulthood. Better than anyone else of his acquaintance, Ian filled Calan's needs in that regard, and he wasn't going to let the opportunity slip by. The fact that the man would leave in a relatively short time meant that there would be no chance to fall in love with him or work to keep his interest hidden from his aunt's notice for long.

He was careful to remain in the back of the throng and didn't dare look in the count's direction at all. This close would prove too uncomfortable and test his ability to hide his interest. Better to bide his time and look for an opportunity to approach the man after the meal. He exchanged brief and polite greetings, then stood with his hands clasped in front of him and staring at the floor. The back of his neck itched in a sudden and inexplicable way. He instinctively looked up to see if there was some approaching danger. That's when his gaze met Ian's straight on. The outrageous man winked at him as he'd done earlier in the day, a very bold move. Calan's mouth dropped open for a second and his cheeks burned before he got himself back under control. He might be trying to be circumspect, but the count obviously was not. That probably came down to the difference between being a powerful man and an orphan dependent on the largesse of a disapproving relative.

Calan managed to avoid Ian and his unnerving attention until the meal began. Once more, he was seated far away from the council members and their illustrious guests. This time, however, he made no effort to catch as many glimpses as possible of the count. Instead, he kept his head down, concentrating on eating and making the occasional small talk with those around him. He knew everyone in the room, having lived among their relatively small community his whole life. Shadow Valley people were mostly happy by nature and good company. If not for the fact that some part of his mind dwelled on what the rest of the evening would hold for him, he would have enjoyed the festive event far more. As it was, once dessert was over and people started leaving the table, his stomach clenched in anticipation mixed with a little dread.

Figuring that the count would be the one to make the bold move necessary to advance their budding acquaintance, Calan quietly left the longhouse by the back door to give them both privacy when the count chose to approach him. He entered the mostly herb garden and breathed in the sweet, fresh night air, enjoying the coolness and quiet compared to the somewhat stuffy and noisy longhouse. As he wandered over to a stone bench, he spied some errant weeds and plucked them out of the ground from habit. He felt Ian's presence behind him and straightened to whirl around. The count stood close, yet not so much as to crowd him, his hands clasped behind his back and a faint smile on his lips.

Calan swallowed hard as he composed himself. His heartbeat raced, and his fingers twitched with nervousness so much that he tucked them behind his back in mimicry of the count's stance. "My lord, you do creep up on a person." He licked his lips before adding, "I thought I walked quietly, but you're like a silent wind."

The man's lips spread in a wider grin. "Forgive me. That's my military training, and to be frank, I assumed you were leading me out here. I didn't mean to startle you...or scare you."

"I'm not scared," Calan hastened to say. "And you're right. I was hoping you'd join me here, away from scrutiny." He dared to give a shy smile himself.

Ian closed the gap between them. "Very clever of you. We are both under the watchful eyes of women who have great influence in our lives."

"My aunt means well." Calan felt the need to defend Celia, even as he wished her to be different, less judgmental.

"As does my sister." Ian was close enough that his wine-laced breath and the heat of his large body wrapped around Calan like a blanket—a comforting one. "And she is very practical and serious in her endeavors. But I, a mere man, am captive to my desires—and what I desire right now is you."

"Oh." Calan couldn't muster anything more coherent than that. As Ian lifted a hand and reached for him, all he could do was close his eyes and lean into the touch.

"You are exquisite." Ian's voice was low and husky. He cupped Calan's face with one hand, running his thumb against Calan's check. "So soft and... inexperienced?"

It took a moment for Calan to realize he'd been asked a question. He opened his eyes to stare into Ian's. They were practically nose-to-nose. "Yes. Is that a problem?" He held his breath waiting for the answer, worried for the first time that the count might not be interested in someone who didn't already know how to please him.

"Not in the least, dear boy."

Relief coursed through him, but he had only a moment to appreciate that feeling before Ian captured his entire attention by lowering his head until their lips touched. It was impossible to keep his eyes open, if for no other reason than rational thought fled the moment the kiss began. It wasn't how he'd imagined it. He'd always expected something ravaging, with lips and teeth and tongue clashing in an effort to consume and dominate. This was a gentle assault, soft and tender. The count treated him as if he were made from glass, their mouths slipping over one another in a slow, lazy dance. His grip on Calan's shoulder was light as he pulled him in closer to his body, although not quite making them touch, which was a shame. Calan wanted to feel the whole of the man. He was sure he must be as hard as Calan was himself, and he'd never felt another man's cock. The lure of it was overwhelming. But when he dared to grab Ian's waist and try to press against him, he held him at bay.

Ian chuckled against Calan's lips. "Eager boy." Pulling away a fraction, he put his forehead against him and sighed. "If we were in a more secluded place, I would give you more. Alas, someone might come along at any time and see us."

"I don't care." Calan was surprised by how husky his own voice sounded.

Ian chuckled again before pecking Calan's forehead and separating them entirely by letting go and stepping back from Calan's hold. "Such a temptation you are. But I won't embarrass or dishonor you that way."

He forced his eyes open and tried not to pout. "There is no shame in this. People seek pleasure with those of their own sex all the time before marriage. It's encouraged, actually, because it means children aren't conceived accidentally. Is it not that way in Moorcondia?" It hadn't occurred to him that what he was seeking from the count would be frowned upon in the man's country.

Now the count laughed. "Have you not heard of our Princes Soren and Ronan being married to other men? It has become quite the rage, actually." He shook his head with a smile. "No, dear boy, what we seek to do is quite acceptable among my people, and I'm glad to hear it is in Shadow Valley. That does not change the fact that public displays of such great…affection are not decorous. It's best done in privacy, and I dare say your aunt would not be pleased to find us in an indelicate state out in the open."

Calan frowned. "That's true." His palms itched with the need to touch the man again, so he made himself bold. "Are you free tomorrow or must you stay with your sister?"

The heated gaze the count sent him told him his efforts were appreciated. "She is well-guarded, even if I sensed danger for her here, which I don't. I find myself rather surplus to requirements and so have all day to do as you wish."

Calan didn't even try to hide his delight, grinning broadly and almost bouncing with anticipation. "Wonderful. I have foraging chores all day, though," he added with a gnaw at his lower lip. "I have to wander in the woods, gathering ingredients that my aunt needs for her potions. It's not very interesting, actually."

Ian surprised him. "I beg to differ. Spending the day outdoors is how I like to occupy my time. I enjoy nature and being with you will make it all the more appealing."

"Really? We can leave after breakfast, if that pleases you."

"*You* please me, Calan. And it will be your day to lead me where you will."

Picturing his usual haunts and how secluded they were, Calan couldn't help but blush.

Chapter Three

Shadow Valley lived up to its name once one was standing under the canopy of the forest. The thick woods were an easy ride from the longhouse. Yet the moment Ian had crossed the thicket line with Calan, leaving the horses hobbled in a field, it felt as if they were in a world of their own. This was the perfect place for a private seduction. It took all his will power not to drop the baskets he carried and pull the boy in for another kiss. The one the previous night had been delightful, yet it had also left him hard and aching for more. He wondered if the boy had understood the effect he'd had on him and how much self-control it had taken not to ravage him on the spot, there where anyone could have come upon them. It was humbling to know that a simple kiss had brought him to his knees. The fact that Calan was not just a virgin, but wholly inexperienced, should give him pause and send him into retreat. Instead, it disturbed him to know he wanted him even more because of it.

When did I become such a letch?

He wasn't being fair to himself. Calan was a grown man, merely untried still at an age when Ian and most men of his acquaintance had known pleasure with others. With his dragon of an aunt always watching out, he probably had had little opportunity to explore sex. And no doubt, Celia's being on the council put the fear of the gods into any man who might think to try his luck with Calan. As a foreigner and a man of power himself, he had no such qualms. His only concern was to not cause Calan any trouble, and these woods presented the best opportunity to do what he and the boy both clearly wanted to do.

"It's very kind of you to carry my baskets." Calan shot a pretty smile over his shoulder.

Ian swung the large, empty wicker cradle he held in one hand. "It's no trouble at all. And I have to justify my presence somehow. Being your porter is a good use of my time." The closed basket he gripped by its handle. "I'm curious to know what's in here, though."

Calan stopped by an old tree and faced him. "That's our lunch, of course. The forest is full of food, but I thought you might like something more refined."

"I'm not picky, but I appreciate the effort and can't wait to see what you've brought."

"We have a ways to go before it's time to eat, but I think you'll like the spot I have picked out for it. I'm surprised you don't have any guards with you, although I'm happy with the privacy."

"The soldiers are for Isabeau and Amalie. I can take care of myself."

"That I can believe." Calan took a knife out of the sheaf at his belt and knelt beside some mushrooms growing at the base of the tree. Unlike the previous day, the boy was dressed in obvious work clothes of simple brown and scarred boots that matched. His lovely hair was pulled back in a severe braid that hung down his back. The hairstyle allowed his beautiful face to be on display, yet Ian wanted to free the strands and run his fingers through them. He assumed there would be an opportunity to do so when they broke for the midday meal. And he would be sure to redo the braid before they returned so that no one would be the wiser.

With deft strokes, Calan severed the mushrooms from the ground and stood to place them in the open basket. "These are good for helping swollen and painful joints. My aunt makes them into a paste and a cordial."

Ian peered at the fungi. "My sister is well-versed in the healing arts. That's why she was chosen to come here by our king, after all. I'm more interested in food cultivation, but I'm beginning to appreciate this side of nature, as well." He let his interest in Calan shine through his gaze and was rewarded by the boy's adorable blush.

Calan looked away as he replaced his knife. "Then I shall try to educate you on as much as I can. It's the least I can do," he added with a coquettish look.

A natural tease, then. Ian didn't mind the boy's boldness. Nor did his dick, which boldly demanded to be let out to play. He mashed the collection basket against his groin to keep it in check. Hard to do, of course, with Calan leading the way, his small backside visible even with his tunic hanging past his waist. To keep himself under control, Ian focused on what the boy was gathering and the tutorial as to why.

The forest turned out to be a veritable marketplace of medicinals — or the raw ingredients that would turn them into such. Calan stopped frequently to gather fungi, plants, tubers and bark. He didn't hesitate in his journey, knowing where he wanted to go, and his sure movements in collecting his specimens confirmed that this was a frequent task. Ian wondered if Celia ever did this herself or had she become dependent on her nephew to labor on her behalf. If so, it would explain her hostile looks thrown in Ian's direction. When Calan had told the woman that Ian would be coming with him, her fury had been barely banked. It occurred to him now, too, that perhaps the woman was worried that Calan would give away the secret to the woman's new and miraculous cordial. If so, Ian wanted to put that fear to rest. Isabeau was tasked with making a treaty to obtain the medicine. He wasn't there as a spy or a thief.

The next time Calan stopped to pluck something up, Ian knelt down next to him. "I trust you know I'm here today to spend time with you because I want you and not as a ploy to pry information out of you."

Calan stopped mid-snip and stared at him. "Of course I do. It never occurred to me that you have ulterior motives. And I wouldn't tell you my people's secrets, anyway. The treaty will be of too great a benefit to them for me to give away that which can be bartered."

When the boy looked down again, obviously uncomfortable with the topic, Ian put the food basket down in order to lift Calan's chin with the side of his finger. "And I would never ask you to do otherwise. Let us agree that we are leaving politics to the politicians while taking some time to please ourselves."

To emphasize his point, Ian gave in to the urge to show the boy some affection. He leaned in to kiss him, intending to keep it light as he had the night before. One touch of their lips, however, broke his control. Dropping the other basket, he hauled Calan in to deepen the kiss. He attacked the boy's mouth as it was meant to be, pressing his tongue inside to taste and conquer. Calan squeaked and stiffened for only a moment before melting into his embrace. Far from being passive, the boy embraced Ian and poured his own passion into the kiss. Before he knew what was happening, Ian found himself sprawled against a nearby tree, Calan in his lap, their bodies pressed together.

Ian's hard cock clashed into Calan's. The obvious sign of the boy's arousal goosed his own, and Ian couldn't resist humping their dicks together. For him, it was merely a way to prime himself for what was to come later. For an untried boy like Calan, the movement proved too much. With a cry muffled by Ian's move, the boy first stiffened, then shuddered as his climax shot through him. Ian held on to him tightly and deepened the kiss, swallowing the sound he wrung out of the boy and using his body to drain him dry.

When it was over, Calan broke the kiss and collapsed into him, his head resting against Ian's chest and breathing as if he'd run a long distance. "Oh my, that was…overwhelming." He panted out the words and clutched at Ian's tunic.

Ian kissed the top of the boy's head. "Apologies, dear boy. I didn't mean to take it that far so soon."

A strangled giggle tore out of Calan. "No apologies needed. It was amazing, although I'm going to need to wash out my trousers before returning home." He lifted his head, his eyes gleaming. "Fortunately, the place I have picked out for our break will permit me to do so." His gaze dropped. "I think our work here is not quite done. You need…"

Ian grabbed Calan's hand before he wormed it between their bodies. "Not necessary. There's plenty of time for me, and the waiting makes it all the more pleasurable."

Calan pouted in obvious disappointment. "You have more willpower than I do, apparently."

"The function of experience and age. I don't have as many orgasms in me as you do on any given day, darling. I like to use up my quota sparingly."

Calan ran his fingers down Ian's cheek. It was like the touch of a butterfly and sent delicious shivers down his spine. "You are hardly old." He moved his hand down to press it against one of Ian's pecs. "And you are very strong — yet also gentle."

Ian roamed his own hands up and down Calan's slender back. "I try to always be careful with those weaker than myself. I will never use my strength to hurt you, Calan." He wasn't sure why he felt the need to say that. There was something vulnerable about this boy. He brought out Ian's protective instincts just as much as Isabeau and Amalie did.

"I'm not afraid of you."

"Good." Ian tucked a few strands of hair that he'd inadvertently tugged from the braid behind Calan's ear. "Always remember that when it comes to what we do together, you are in control. We go at your pace and do only what you are comfortable with."

"Oh." Calan sighed and his face took on a dreamy look. "I want to do it all in what little time we have with each other."

Ignoring the unexpected jolt he felt at the reminder of how short his visit was going to be, Ian gave Calan a reassuring smile. "And so we shall. Now, we should continue."

As hard as it was to let go of the warm bundle in his lap, Ian lifted Calan off him and helped him to his feet as he stood himself. He brushed the leaves and dirt off his backside and tried not to look at Calan's debauched lips. It was entirely too hard to resist the boy and to risk the temptation. Some of the items had spilled from the basket when he'd dropped it. He quickly put everything to rights and nodded. "What's next?"

Calan had an impish look on his face when he opened his mouth, then with a shrug, turned sober. "This way."

It was more of the same, except Calan's pace increased and he gathered fewer items. They broke free of the tree line to a gleaming lake before them. It took a moment to recognize the spot was the one where he'd first spied Calan on the journey into Shadow Valley.

Calan stopped beside a natural path that led up to the top of the overhanging rock. "How about a swim before we eat?"

"An excellent idea." Ian put the baskets down and nearly stumbled as he caught sight of Calan stripping.

Of course, they needed to take off their clothing before entering the lake, but despite his vast experience with men and his previous viewing of Calan's body, he wasn't prepared for the staggering effect of seeing him naked up close. The boy's body was perfectly proportioned, his limbs slender and toned, his ass tight and pert and his cock...utterly delicious looking as it jutted out with renewed arousal.

Calan stood peering back at him with a sly expression. "Aren't you going to take off your clothes?"

Ian nodded. "As soon as I can manage to do so without tripping over my tongue. You are a veritable feast, my dear, for my eyes."

"You have me at a disadvantage, my lord."

"Ah. My apologies." Ian unbuckled his sword belt and put it near the baskets before yanking off his tunic. This he tossed with less care, as he did with his boots and trousers. Soon, he stood as naked and aroused as Calan. He watched the boy taking in the sight of him, hoping his large physique and dick weren't overwhelming.

Calan licked his lower lip before saying, "You are everything I imagined my first lover to be. I want to touch you all over."

Ian was humbled by the observation. "Consider it your toy. Do as you wish with it. Although let us at least swim first. I need the cooling down or I fear my desire for you will overtake my reason."

"As you wish, my lord." Calan scampered up the rest of the path, obviously something he did routinely. At the top of the rock, he looked back at Ian over his shoulder before diving into the clear water below.

Ian didn't hesitate to follow. The bracing water cooled his blood the moment he hit it, yet the first thing he did was open his eyes and search out his quarry.

* * * *

Calan swam under the water in his usual way, except this time he knew he wasn't alone. Someone chased after him, and knowing who it was turned it into an enticing game of cat and mouse. When long, hard arms encircled his waist, he was ready for it. He twisted within the slick embrace until he was face-to-face with the count. Even through the curtain of water, he could see the hunger in the man's eyes. His lungs burned with the need for air, yet he was tempted to kiss his captor. Ian didn't stop him from pressing their mouths together but kicked them upward while they meshed their lips.

They broke the surface with a mutual sputter. Then Calan was being held tightly against Ian, their mouths once more crushing each other. They kept on kissing while Ian kicked them over to the shore. Calan wrapped his legs around the man's waist, letting him do all the work, certain that he could. The count's strength was as impressive as any laborer Calan had ever seen. And his cock? Well, that was the stuff of dreams. Calan had seen lots of men naked before. From what he'd dared peek at, none had the kind of manhood that Ian sported. The thought of it entering his body made his hole clench. It would be hard to take, but he had brought some cream to ease the way. That was assuming the man would mount him that afternoon. *Perhaps not.* Ian's obvious concern for him meant he might take matters more slowly than that.

Damn it.

Ian still held him, nibbling his mouth, jaw and even his earlobe as he walked out of the lake. Without the cool water to impede their dicks, they had both become fully aroused by the time Ian sat down on a large, flat rock. Calan straddled his lap, surprised by his own boldness. He was normally reticent around others, but there was something about Ian that broke through his barrier of wariness of getting close to someone else. It felt right and natural to be here, in this man's arms with their hard cocks brushing each other. The sparks of pleasure made him shiver and moan. He clenched his fingers into Ian's heavily muscled shoulders and tried to press as close to the man as he could.

The count eased his efforts by cupping his ass with both hands and lifting him up and down in a slow ride that mashed and ground their dicks together. It took only a few times before Calan's control broke. He came with a rush that had him crying out loudly enough to startle birds from the trees. Ian crushed his mouth with a deep kiss, swallowing his howls while continuing to hump their bodies. Within seconds more, Calan felt a splash of warmth against his belly and a deep growl echoed down his throat. The count shuddered from his climax—a movement that left Calan feeling oddly powerful. *I did that to him.* It was his first sexual experience with another person, and he hadn't been prepared for how overwhelmingly emotional it would be.

Ian abruptly ended the kiss and parted their bodies. "What's this? Are you all right?" He brushed his thumbs under Calan's eyes. "Tell me why you're crying."

Calan fluttered his eyes open and saw worry in the count's gaze. "I-I didn't know I was." He batted his lashes as more tears leaked out. "How very strange." He threw himself at the man's chest and hugged him tightly.

Ian wrapped his arms around him in return and rocked him gently, although this time there was nothing sexual about it. "I didn't mean to frighten you. It was too much too soon, I'm afraid."

Calan shook his head. "No. No, it was wonderful. I'm just being a ninny. You're my first, you know—for everything. These are happy tears."

Ian ran his palm in slow circles around his back, a soothing gesture that would have been parental if not for the way it made his cock start to harden again. The count was also becoming aroused, his large dick swelling against Calan's hip. They might have repeated the dry humping except Ian stood abruptly and walked them both into the chilly lake water. Then the man lowered Calan to his feet and forced them apart, although he kept one hand on his waist while washing cum off them both. When he was done, he led Calan back to the shore.

"I think it's time for luncheon and a talk." Letting go of Calan, he squatted by the basket and opened it. He pulled out the thin quilt that was intended to serve as a blanket. "You thought of everything, I see." He tipped his head in Calan's direction. "Do you want to sit on the grass or the rock?"

Feeling a bit shy, Calan tucked his loosened and wet hair behind his ears and stared at the ground. "The grass, please."

Ian spread out the quilt with a quick snap of his wrists and smoothed it with his hands before waving Calan to take a seat. He knelt beside him and peered into the basket. "Let's see what we have."

"It's nothing much." The council had gone to great lengths to feast their Moorcondian visitors with opulent food. Normally, they ate plainly, and he worried now that his choice of food would pale in comparison to what the count was used to having.

"I beg to differ." Ian pulled out thick sandwiches of ham, smothered with a strong mustard that Calan had made himself. "This is the perfect meal after so much exercise." He winked at him.

Calan knew he blushed. This playfulness after intimacy was a bit stunning. He didn't seem able to control his emotions. "There's cider to wash it down and stalks of celery and apples."

Ian laid all the meal on the quilt, then pulled out a small pot. "Is this a condiment?"

Mortified, Calan lunged to snatch it from his hands. "No. It's not. It's, um, nothing." He put it behind his back. His cheeks were on fire, and he dared not look at the count.

Leaning toward him, Ian cupped Calan's chin and forced it up. "My dear, you need not ever be embarrassed in front of me. I applaud your forethought, although regrettably, we'll not be in need of any lubricant this afternoon."

Disappointment overrode his awkwardness. "Why not?"

"Because you're not ready."

Now Calan frowned. "I am so. I've been ready for a while and only lacked the opportunity. I want you."

The count's face broke out into a smile. "A delightful confession, and I can assure you that I am of the same inclination. However," he added, rising with his cock once more thickening, "you're first time being breached by a man must be done with care. Not something to be done in haste outdoors." He walked over to his clothing and impressively stuffed his legs and his dick back into his trousers. "And as you've already seen, there is much pleasure to be had with other, less…invasive ways." He smiled so charmingly as he sat across from him that Calan couldn't help doing the same.

"I suppose you're right. It was amazing what you did for me. I'm sorry if my tears gave you the wrong impression." He frowned again as he handed a sandwich over to Ian. "I guess I was overwhelmed by the experience. I'm not used to being close to people," he confessed before taking a big bite of his own sandwich.

"You spend a lot of time alone, don't you?"

Calan swallowed his mouthful before answering. "It depends on how you see it. I'm always with the animals of the forest. They are good company."

"I understand." Ian bit off nearly half the sandwich and moaned. It was almost the same sound he made when he came. "This is delicious."

"I'm glad you like it. The mustard is my own recipe and my aunt baked the bread, but neither of us can take credit for the ham. Our neighbor is a hog farmer. We get all our meat from others. I'm no good at animal husbandry. The caring of them is fine. The ending of them, not so much. Fishing is too hard for me, let alone slaughtering animals."

Ian nodded. "I understand. It's hard for me, too, but I never ask anything of those who work my lands that I can't do myself." He stuffed the remainder of his sandwich into his mouth before picking up another one.

Calan nibbled on his own, having a small stomach that rarely needed more than he'd already eaten. "You don't mean to say you work beside your people all the time?"

Ian nodded as he chewed. "That's exactly what I mean. We labor together almost every day all year round. I love the physical nature of it and being outside." He shrugged. "And, how else would I occupy my time?"

"I guess I imagined that Moorcondian nobility spend their days having fun."

Ian grinned broadly. "Working the land *is* fun, although I must confess I'm different from the average man of my class. And I enjoy reading and playing cards and such during the winter months when there's less to do." He shrugged again. "I don't like idleness, and court life is excruciatingly boring, so I stay at home most of the time. I also travel to visit my sister and niece as often as I can, but that's the extent of my wanderings."

"You're here now." Calan finished his sandwich and grabbed a stalk of celery to clean his teeth. "Shadow Valley is a long way to come."

"I'm here for my sister. Now she's excellent at maneuvering around the court and other diplomatic matters, as well as healing. There was no better choice for our king to make. I just can't help worrying about her, that's all. So there was no question I was going to accompany her."

"She's perfectly safe here, you know. My people might be hesitant about sharing our medicinals, but we are not dangerous unless provoked."

Ian snatched his own celery before lounging down on one elbow. "I know. That's why I'm perfectly comfortable spending this glorious day with you and not her." The suggestive look he gave Calan caused the predictable reaction.

He wrapped his arms around his waist in a futile effort to hide his erection. "You need to stop doing that unless you want to use the cream."

The count actually laughed and moved with a dizzying swiftness, pressing Calan onto his back and holding him there by the hips. "I told you there are other ways to give pleasure that don't involve having sufficient time to take great care. You've seen one. Let me show you another."

With his heart threatening to burst, Calan could only nod. Then he slammed his eyes shut as Ian took his cock into his mouth. It was shocking in its intensity—his entire dick being swallowed up by a soft warmth that nevertheless gripped him like a vise. He clenched at the blanket hard enough to make his hands hurt. Staccato pants escaped his mouth and a keening noise welled up from his throat. The sensations of being sucked and licked overloaded him, leaving his thoughts to be consumed by a dizzy maelstrom. He tossed his head back and forth and bucked into Ian's mouth, demanding…he didn't know what. That was until the man swallowed. Then he understood what he'd needed. That last claiming of his cock sent him over the edge. He yelled into the sky above him and shook as the orgasm rushed through him.

The next thing he knew, Calan found himself lying in Ian's arms. The man held him in a light embrace, stroking his arm. He snuggled against Ian and yawned against the back of his own hand.

"I think I need a nap." He giggled at the notion. His energy was usually boundless.

Ian kissed the top of his head. "Do so. I have you, my dear, and promise you are safe with me."

"I know." As silly as it might seem to trust someone so completely after such a short acquaintance, there was no denying the truth of it.

* * * *

"I can't believe I slept so long." Calan rushed to dress, the position of the sun telling him time was short for them to return before the evening meal. They'd have to push their horses to gallop, which he liked doing anyway.

The count lounged on the blanket, eating an apple, and given that he was already clothed, at his ease. "You were dead to the world, and I didn't have the heart to wake you. And there is plenty of time. I doubt we've even been missed."

Knowing his aunt as he did, Calan was of a different opinion. But he didn't want to make Ian feel guilty, and it had been wonderful to wake in the man's arms. "There's a shorter path we can take back to where we left the horses now that I'm not foraging." He righted his clothing, then started to disentangle his hair to re-braid it.

"Let me do that."

Calan looked skeptically at the man. "You want to do my hair?"

Ian smiled. "Why not?"

With a shrug, Calan sat down with his back to the count. "If you wish." He was thrilled, actually, at the thought of it. There was something intimate in the simple act of touching another's hair. To his surprise, the count proved adept at plaiting. "How are you so good at this?"

"Oh, I used to do Isabeau's all the time."

"Didn't she have a maid or something for that?"

"Yes, but not outside where we would spend the day playing. It might be hard to believe now, but that proper woman you met used to chase after me when we were children, determined to do everything I was. Our father frowned upon such activities for girls, however, so we had to make her as presentable as possible when we returned to the manor so that he wouldn't know what she'd been up to. Happily, she has raised Amalie differently, although I like to keep my hand in by braiding my niece's hair on occasion. There."

Calan ran his hand down the braid and looked over his shoulder. "I couldn't have done a better job myself. Thank you." He dared to peck Ian on the lips and was tempted to do more, except the sun wasn't going to wait on its journey down. "We need to hurry."

Ian had already packed up the basket and grabbed it and the wicker cradle to follow Calan on the shorter path. As they passed the cave opening near the outcrop of rock, the man remarked on it. "That looks like a fun place to explore."

Calan nearly stumbled as he realized he'd brought the count to the one place he shouldn't have. He recovered as quickly as he could and tried to sound casual as he hurried on. "Oh, it is. I'll show it to you sometime, if you like." He held his breath, hoping Ian would let the topic go.

"That might be...interesting." There was something in the man's tone that caused unease.

Calan didn't dare dwell on it further, however, and raced back to the village.

Chapter Four

"Honestly, Ian, you're like a child who can't tell time."

Ian stood under his sister's withering glare, trying not to squirm. "I was back in plenty of time, Isabeau. As you can see, I'm ready to go to the banquet." He did not add, because he liked his balls to remain right where they were, that it was *he* who had waited for *her* to be ready.

Isabeau harrumphed. "I'm not going to mention how you spent the entire afternoon with that boy, doing the gods know what."

Once again, he didn't point out that she had, in fact, just spoke of that very thing. "He was showing me his foraging. It was quite informative, actually."

His sister stopped in her tracks and eyed him intently. "He didn't happen to give you any information about the ingredients for their new cordial, did he?"

"No, of course not. He's loyal to his people and not stupid." He kept to himself the encounter with the cave by the lake. He'd sensed in Calan's change in demeanor that there was something there he hadn't intended to show. Whether it was about this new medicine or not remained to be seen, but Ian wasn't going to break the boy's budding trust in him by pushing the matter. It had been humbling the way Calan had responded to his touch and had lain trustingly in his arms for a few hours.

"I suppose it was too much to hope for." Isabeau continued on her way.

Ian matched her dainty steps. "How did the day's negotiation go?"

"Well enough. They are wary, to be sure, and I've had to prove my skills as a healer to them. We spent most of the time discussing various tonics, cordials and potions. Our knowledge of such overlaps almost completely…if you discount their latest concoction, that is."

All those words sounded the same to him, and whatever nuances they had for healers, he knew that his sister could stand up with the best of them. "Their many generations of isolation is a hard thing for them to get over, I imagine."

Isabeau shot him a look of disdain. "Of course it is. The king has authorized me to offer them a very valuable treaty, but they seem almost indifferent to its benefits. I've laid out in plain terms what Moorcondia will give them, but they showed no signs that they were impressed with its value, which is substantial. The king isn't driving a hard bargain here. The council should be jumping at the opportunity to obtain such benefits. One gets the impression, however, that they want a more personal connection.

"It reminds me of when I visited the Truehearts for the first time. Richard's family was unfailingly polite, and yet I knew I was being tested to see if I was worthy of him and would fit nicely into their lives." She shuddered theatrically. "It was almost unbearably stressful until he took me into his arms one night, kissed me and said we suited each other very well. After that, nothing seemed to matter. I started to fall in love with him at that moment."

Knowing that the marriage had been arrange by their parents, and even seeing that his sister had been happy with her husband, it was good to hear for the first time, that she'd also loved the man. It was no wonder she mourned him still and refused to entertain any other men in her life. And while both families had benefited economically from the marital bond, the emotional glue had been the best binder of the arrangement. The strength of a personal connection, as Isabeau had described it, was why marriages often came with treaties. The import of his thoughts caused him to come to a dead stop.

No. That would be ridiculous. This treaty is being forged by the exchange of goods only. Even as he tried to dissuade himself of his burgeoning plan, Isabeau's words in the carriage popped into his head. *A marriage would do wonders for a treaty…*

Isabeau stopped with him and gasped. "For goodness' sake, Ian, what is it?"

He shook his head and got his feet moving again. "Nothing. Sorry."

But it was *not* 'nothing'. The proof of it was standing right inside the longhouse by Councilwoman Celia's side. At Isabeau's entrance, all eyes turned to her, and by extension, to him. There was only one person whose gaze mattered, however. He stared at Calan as he followed his sister. Everything inside him tightened. It wasn't merely arousal, although that was terribly evident by the cramp in his cock and balls. The reaction was more holistic than that, as if every fiber of his being were on high alert. It was the feeling of going into battle. He'd done very little fighting in his life, but enough for him to recognize his body's response. In theory, there was nothing dangerous about his situation, yet he couldn't quite help believing that his life was on a path not of his making.

He stopped in front of the council members and managed to murmur polite greetings to them all before once again, focusing on Calan. "It's good to see you. You seem quite refreshed, despite our long day." It wasn't perhaps fair of him, but the blush that rose on the boy's cheeks pleased him immensely. Calan wore his emotions on his sleeve more than most.

Calan angled away from his aunt. "Good evening, my lord. I hope you enjoyed my hospitality, simple as it was."

The little minx was flirting in his own way. "Indeed I did. It was very enlightening to explore the beauty of your country and its endless bounty."

Celia broke in before Calan could respond, grabbing the boy by his arm. "Time to sit. Remember your place, Calan." In emphasis of her double meaning, she glared at Ian before propelling her nephew forward.

"Yes, Aunt." Calan's tone was meek, but he managed to shoot Ian a sly smile before walking away.

Celia was not done, however. With everyone going to settle at the table, they were alone for the first time. She narrowed her eyes at him. "You would do well to remember that you are a guest here, Count Charteris, and on sufferance because of your sister's diplomatic standing. My nephew is a young and impressionable innocent, not a plaything to amuse yourself with."

Ian worked to keep his tone civil, his hackles rising. "I assure you, madam, that I understand completely what the situation is. Calan's welfare is of the utmost importance to me."

"It best be, because I will be the one to pick up the pieces once you have left." With that, she turned on her heel and sailed away.

Ian remained frozen to the spot for a few seconds as his brain insisted on revisiting the path of his previous thoughts. *There will be nothing to pick up if he leaves with me.* No, the idea was insane on the face of it. He'd known the boy for little more than a minute, and the intimacy they'd shared had clearly impacted Calan more strongly than Ian had expected. He was playing with emotional fire, and the best thing to do would be to heed Celia's warning and back off. And yet, he couldn't help thinking of Isabeau and Richard, making a happy life and home together on a short acquaintance. That wasn't unusual for marriages in general, at least not in Moorcondia. Mutual respect and enjoying each other's company could grow after the wedding and made for a solid foundation if love never bloomed between them. There was a lot to be said for physical compatibility, as well, and there was no denying how much Calan and he had enjoyed each other.

"It's madness."

A passing servant stopped. "Your pardon, my lord, did you need something?"

Ian couldn't help but send his gaze in Calan's direction. "Yes, it seems as if I do."

* * * *

"You've been avoiding me."

Ian looked up from where he'd been inspecting the maze fountain's mechanism, trying not to look too smug over how his ploy had worked. "Not at all, my dear. I've merely showed discretion while so many prying eyes surrounded us. I don't want to hurt your reputation or give your aunt reason to chastise you. I am, however," he added, stepping toward Calan and running a hand over his head, "delighted that you followed me."

Calan's coquettish grin was easy to see in the moon-lit night. "As I'm sure you knew I would."

"Well, I had hoped," Ian said on a sigh right before gently kissing the boy. He wanted so much more, but they weren't that isolated. Breaking off the kiss, he satisfied himself by roaming his hands up and down Calan's arms. "You're very beautiful."

Calan's eyes were at half-mast. "Can boys be beautiful? I thought that only applied to girls."

"Beauty knows no gender and isn't reserved for people. It's all around us in many things of nature. Someone who spends as much time enjoying the natural world knows that, surely." A slight trembling of the boy's body could be felt. Ian knew he aroused them both and probably should step away. He simply couldn't. His desire for Calan was growing, and his need for him becoming more insistent.

"Hmm, I suppose that's true. I've just never thought of myself as such, and you're right, no one has complimented me like that. I don't think they would dare, but you are brave enough to do whatever you please, aren't you, Count? It's one of the things I find compelling about you—your strength and courage, your raw, masculine power."

Amused at the description, Ian cupped the boy's face and ran a thumb along one cheekbone. "You have quite a flattering view of me. I am, at heart, a farmer. But it is true that I have an irritating tendency to go after what I want…and get it."

Calan turned his face into Ian's palm and moaned. "Do you want me?"

"Very much so. Have I been less than clear on that point?" Every fiber of his being was tight with need. His cock acted as if it hadn't been seen to all day, urgent in its hardness. A thought flashed through him that there were plenty of isolated parts of the maze where he might lie Calan down and…

"Then kiss me some more."

Ian gave in to the soft demand, tugging the boy in flush against him and capturing his lips once more with urgency. As he plundered Calan's mouth, he cupped his small ass for leverage to lift him off the ground to better align their groins. Calan helped by wrapping his legs around Ian's waist. Once again, their hard dicks mated, layers of clothing frustratingly muting their efforts. It didn't matter. Calan clutched Ian's shoulders and squeezed his thighs, increasing the friction of their bodies colliding by rolling his slender hips. It took mere seconds before they were sending their stifled cries down each other's throats. They broke the kiss and stood panting. When Ian's legs threatened to give out, he moved them both to sit on the edge of the fountain.

Calan leaned his head against Ian's chest and shuddered. "I have no control when you touch me."

Ian chuckled. "I have a similar problem with you."

He tightened his grip on the boy's arm, a flood of emotion swamping him suddenly. The feeling amplified the burgeoning plan he'd been kicking around in his head since they'd returned from their forest romp. It didn't seem so far-fetched at the moment and the feeling that he wasn't quite in control of his own destiny not disconcerting after all. In fact, the idea was quickly crystalizing as the best path forward, both diplomatically and personally. *Will Calan agree?* Part of him said it didn't matter, that the boy would do what he was told. But that wasn't how he wanted it to be. What made these interludes amazing was their mutual eagerness. He didn't want someone in his bed who was there only out of duty. *I will convince him.*

"I wish I could invite you back to my room." Calan lifted his head. "Or, I could go to yours. I assume the council has given you a private space."

Oh, that was too tempting. The thought of carrying the boy to his bed and making love to him was overwhelming. It was also impossible. "That would be very rude of me. While I have a separate room, I am quartered in a house with my family and their servants, not to mention the dozens of guards. There would be no way for me to sneak you in with me. Word would spread, and I'm sure the council would frown upon such open dalliance. I know my sister would take a strip out of my hide."

Reluctantly, Ian stood them both up before his better judgment was overruled by his cock. Calan's mew of disappoint made him smile. "Now, now, there is always tomorrow. We can have another picnic."

Calan shook his head. "I'm sorry, we can't. I have to spend the day in my aunt's workshop, processing what we foraged today. Everything I gathered must be tended to before it rots. Some of it needs to be hung up to dry and the rest should be ground into paste. It takes all day to do so." He bowed his head in obvious disappointment.

Touched by the display, Ian bent to catch the boy's eye. "Then I shall sit in a corner and watch you work…if you are amenable to my company?"

Calan's eyes flashed along with a grin. "Of course I am." His lips drooped. "You'll be bored, though."

Ian nearly laughed at the suggestion. "Nonsense. I find you endlessly fascinating, darling boy. I suspect I would be entertained watching you paint a fence."

Calan rolled his eyes. "You are quick with honeyed words, my lord, but I will take them at face value because I enjoy spending time with you, too." He looked at the path they'd both used to reach the center of the maze. "I must be going. Surely the others are leaving the banquet at this point, and I want to beat my aunt home so that she doesn't see how wet I am."

A wave of possessiveness crashed over Ian. He liked the thought of others knowing how he'd brought the boy to climax, but it was crass and primitive of him to want it. Calan didn't need the embarrassment of it all. Taking the boy by the hand, he led him out of the maze. Seeing no one about, he sent him on his way with a quick kiss and a promise. "I will see you tomorrow."

Calan gave one last look over his shoulder as he hurried away, leaving Ian to take a moment himself to make sure his own orgasm wasn't obvious. Thank the gods for the layers of good clothing that his station demanded he wear for such formal occasions. Nothing of his interlude with Calan showed. And his timing was perfect. Isabeau was still making her good-byes to

Fennic outside the longhouse when he arrived to escort her back to their lodgings.

Isabeau gave him the fisheye. "Taking the night air, brother?"

With his hands clasped in front of him—just in case an extra barrier was needed—Ian flashed her a bright smile. "Yes, it's a lovely evening."

She narrowed her gaze at him, seeing too much for his comfort. "Hmm." She turned back to Fennic and curtsied. "I look forward to continuing our discussions tomorrow."

Ian fell into step beside his sister as she left, six soldiers surrounding them, as always, for Isabeau's protection. He hoped that the fact that they weren't alone would be enough to make her hold her tongue. And at first, she said nothing, giving him hope that he wouldn't have to answer any awkward questions.

"You smell like a brothel."

He sighed inwardly, glaring at one of the guards who hadn't managed to stifle a smirk. It was too much to expect she hadn't noticed what he'd been up to or would let the matter slide. "That's not a very ladylike observation, Isabeau. How would you know what a bawdy house smells like, anyway? And as it happens, you're wrong. I do *not*."

"Huh! Well, I suppose I must bow to your superior knowledge when it comes to such matters, but I do know the scent of sex. You better hope that poor boy has slipped past his aunt before she gets a whiff of him. Have you no self-control?"

"Apparently not." He let out an audible sigh. "He's a temptation I cannot resist, and it's more than merely physical. I enjoy his company. I'm going to spend the day with him tomorrow while he prepares the ingredients he foraged today." When his sister turned her head to give him an appraising stare, he quickly qualified his intent. "And I won't be there to wheedle information out of him."

She waved the suggestion away. "No, of course not. You are more honorable than that. I am disappointed in myself for even thinking of it. It's just frustrating negotiating with these people. I had hoped it would be easier than this. Moorcondia has so much to offer. I thought I had a great deal to entice them."

It was on the tip of his tongue to voice his possible path forward. He held it, though, because more than anyone, Calan deserved to be the one to hear it first. If the boy weren't willing, then that would be the end of it. The idea that he might not be caused a pit to form in his stomach. Surprised at his reaction, he rubbed a hand across his abdomen and stayed silent for the rest of the way.

* * * *

Calan froze at the sound of footsteps approaching his door. As he lay in the dark, he pictured his aunt listening for any hint of noise coming from his room. This was an old pattern. The woman had always hated giving him any kind of privacy, preferring instead to insert herself into every part of his life. But he'd learned long ago that if he snuffed out the candles and stayed quiet, she would assume he slept and move on. This night was no different. After a few seconds, she walked away. He waited a little while longer before sliding his fingers up the shaft of his already hard cock. Not even Celia's presence had been able to diminish his arousal.

The vision of Ian was too strong, as was the memory of everything the man had done to him that day.

He shuddered at his own touch, reveling in the pleasure it brought him while calling up visions of his cock embedded in Ian's mouth. Using actual experience instead of fantasies to egg on his orgasm was far better than what he was used to when gratifying himself. Now he truly knew what it was like to have another man's hands on him, to be sucked dry, to be held and kissed. He couldn't go back to his own imagination to find satisfaction ever again. He needed to be with a man. He needed to be with *Ian*.

Calan gripped the base of his cock tightly to choke off the climax that threatened to erupt too quickly. He wanted to make this last. It didn't matter how often he'd come that day. He wanted more, was primed for it, as if he'd never orgasmed before in his life. Such was the lasting effect of a powerful lover. He felt as if the man had somehow infused part of his virility into him. His relative peace and calm at being a young man living with his commanding aunt was fraying. There was a restlessness in him now. Nothing about his life was enough. All that mattered was being with the count again.

He sucked on two fingers before raising his hips and pressing them against his hole. The burn that came from sliding them in only added to his pleasure. He fucked himself, imagining that it was Ian's dick doing so and jerked his shaft with hard, sure strokes. The orgasm ripped through him within seconds, causing him to levitate his lower half off his mattress. He nearly bit his lip bloody holding back a cry that threatened to blow the roof off. Jamming his fingers in as far as they could go, he scraped against his prostate to goose the last drops of cum out of his cock. When it was over, he lay panting in the dark, still clenching his shaft and fingers remaining half in his hole. Only a day ago, this would have been the perfect ending to his evening. He would have slept soundly and started the next day as his happy self. Now, it was almost cruel in how it lacked something vital. This self-pleasuring was apparently a pale imitation of what sex could truly be.

Nevertheless, lethargy took hold of him. With slow movements, he forced himself to clean up using a rag he kept for this very purpose. No cum would stain his sheets, and he'd already washed his tunic and trousers of the evidence of what he'd shared with Ian at the fountain. He wondered if the count was bothered by what those who saw to his laundry knew he'd been up to. Probably not. A man like Ian could do as he liked, and no one would think twice about his seeking pleasure with anyone at any time. As he drifted off to sleep, Calan fantasized about what it would be like to live like such a man—not as him, of course, but as his lover. To be free and open had not been something he'd dared dream of. Now, he couldn't help but do so.

* * * *

Calan felt only a little guilty about not asking his aunt's permission to have Ian with him in the workshop. He rationalized it by thinking she had the council negotiations on her mind and didn't need the distraction of something so trivial. It wasn't as if he were going to spill all the secrets of his aunt's potions to the count, after all. He doubted the man would even understand half of what he would say, and Calan could be circumspect when necessary. Besides, Ian was too honorable to use Calan as a means to ferret out information. *Isn't he?* Yes, he was certain that he was right about the man's character. Despite being acquainted for only a few days, he trusted the count, whether it made sense or not. It was a gut-level instinct, and Calan had always been right to go with that feeling in the past. Of course, that was with plants. People were different—and yet not so much that he wasn't sure of his perception.

None of that mattered anyway, because the sight of the man approaching him outside the front doors of the longhouse threw all rational thought out of his head and instinct was supplanted by pure desire. His heart thumped like a dog's tail with happiness and his never-tiring dick stirred with interest. He'd dared to make himself come that morning to help keep himself in check. Apparently his cock hadn't understood the purpose of the exercise. He was as hard and aching as ever.

Ian smiled at him knowingly. "Good morning, Calan." Then, in a lower voice, he said, "I missed you, too."

With lots of people milling around them, Calan feared his face would betray him. He looked at the ground. "You are incorrigible, my lord."

"Guilty. But I thought that was one of the things you like about me."

Calan gasped, yet also smiled. "I must get on. There's lots of work to do today. I trust you will behave yourself while I do so." He started walking toward home.

Ian fell into step beside him with his hands clasped behind his back as he was want to. "Of course, and I assume you will forgive me when I don't."

Before Calan could muster a response to that outrageous statement, someone called his name. Fredric, a widower more than twice his age who had made his interest in him known, came striding up to him with an obvious wheel of cheese wrapped in burlap tucked under his arm.

He stopped in front of him with a wide grin. "Calan, I'm glad I caught you. I wanted you to have the first sample of my latest batch." The farmer held out the cheese as if offering him something of great value. And it was. Fredric might be a bit of a letch, but he did make excellent food from his dairy cows' milk.

Calan took the offering. "Thank you, Fredric. Aunt Celia will be pleased to have it...and so am I," he hastily added.

Fredric cast his gaze at Ian, who loomed by Calan's side. "Of course, we of Shadow Valley take care of our own." He rotated one shoulder. "I'll be needing some more of that cream for my bursitis, if you don't mind. I'm running low."

"Sure thing." Calan tried for a friendly smile with no inuendo. "Come to my aunt's workshop any time." *Just not today.*

Ian plucked the wheel out of Calan's hands without warning. "I'll carry that for you." He sniffed at it. "Smells delicious, Master Fredric. Perhaps I can impose upon Calan to make me a sandwich of it for luncheon."

Fredric's eyes narrowed for a moment before he took a step back. "I'll come around another day when you're not...entertaining." With that, he turned on his heel and strode off.

Calan eyed Ian. "Did you just mark me as your territory or something?"

Ian blinked at him slowly. "Did I? How presumptuous of me. That old goat would be better suited to court your aunt than you, anyway."

Is he jealous? The idea pleased him immensely. "I have no interest in him, although he does make excellent dairy products." He continued walking. "Cheese and tomato sandwiches sound like a good idea. First, however, we have work to do."

Calan hadn't expected the villagers to be as curious as they were while they headed home. While no one was rude about it, their furtive gazes were obvious to him. He supposed the count attracted attention wherever he went simply because of his commanding size and presence. Naturally, people would wonder why the Moorcondian was accompanying him, and word would get back to Celia. He decided it didn't matter. There was nothing shameful in what he did, and the pleasure of spending the day with the man overrode all other considerations.

When they arrived, Calan felt suddenly nervous and shy. Compared to where the count must live, Celia's humble home could not be impressive. He headed straight for the outside door of the adjoining shed instead of entering through the house. Here, there was comfort. The scents of drying flowers filled the room, with the underlying pungency of fungi lending any earthy smell. No matter what, Calan was proud of this space. What he and his aunt achieved here was valuable to their people. He shut the door behind them and watched as Ian took a walk around the room, gazing at everything.

"This is marvelous." Ian turned to look at him. "You know there must be a similar place on my own estate, and naturally Isabeau has a room in Truehart Manor where she works. But I've never actually thought to see either space before. I guess my love of farming hasn't extended to this part of it." He gave Calan a hungry smile. "That's changed. I find myself suddenly fascinated." Holding up the cheese, he asked, "Where should I put this?"

"I'll take it." Calan went to relieve Ian of his burden and found it being lifted out of his reach.

"I want a kiss first."

Calan rolled his eyes. "Very well, although I'm not sure it constitutes much of a payment, given that I want it just as much." To prove it, he stood on his toes and kissed the man.

He'd intended to make it brief, but Ian had other ideas. Before Calan knew what was happening, he was being crushed by one arm against the man's hard chest. Ian snaked his tongue into his mouth, exploring it, as always, as if it had never been there before. By the time Ian let him go, Calan was dizzy with breathlessness.

He leaned against Ian for a moment before taking the now reachable wheel of cheese. "Having you here is a bad idea, it seems." He put the cheese on a nearby table and headed for the storage area for what he'd gathered the previous day.

"I promise I shall behave myself from this moment on."

Calan glanced over his shoulder. "I'm not sure I believe you. Worse, I don't think I care." With a chuckle, he added, "Sit over on that stool and don't be a distraction, my lord. If you're very good, I'll give you a treat after lunch." How he dared to be so bold, he couldn't fathom. It didn't matter anyway. Ian's low chuckle was the reward he was looking for.

Chapter Five

Since childhood, Ian had had a hard time sitting still. It was in his nature to be active, and that meant being outside, working from sunrise to sunset. Staying in one spot for long made him antsy, and yet, as he sat on the ass-bruising stool, watching Calan work, he had never felt more content. Better yet, as he tied up bundles of flowers and ground fungi and tubers into fine granules and pastes, Calan kept up a running tutorial of what he was doing and why. He taught Ian the various uses of what he worked with, as well. It was all fascinating to him, because it was Calan who was providing the instruction. The few occasions in which Isabeau had tried to engage him on the topic of medicinals, he'd nearly been speechless in moments. This was different. Everything was. The sudden and strange turn of events in his life was unsettling, yet he felt no need to fight it anymore.

"It must have taken you a long time to learn all this from your aunt."

Calan pressed and twisted a pestle into its mortar. "Not really. I guess I have a natural affinity to it. Most of the process and formulas are well-known, handed down by generations of healers and apothecaries. My aunt and I aren't the only ones in Shadow Valley—or even in this village—who practice these professions, either. But I like exploring for new things and, well, the plants seem to talk to me. I look at stuff and get a sense of what it might be able to do."

The boy shrugged as he judged his latest effort done and poured the ground material into a glass that he stoppered up and put on a shelf. "I can honestly say that if I had been given a choice to do anything with my life, this would have been it. Although, I wouldn't have chosen to be a healer as such. I struggle with having a good bedside manner. I'm at my best here, making the things that healers can use."

"Do you ever think of traveling outside of Shadow Valley to find new ingredients?" This was the topic he'd wanted to raise from the beginning of the day. He held his breath waiting for an answer. If Calan couldn't conceive of leaving home, Ian's budding plan would die on the vine.

Calan cocked his head and stared at a distant point before answering. "I have, actually. There is always something new to discover, and I can imagine the world is filled with lots of possibilities. Environment matters to plants, and Shadow Valley's is only one kind of climate, I should think. Why do you ask? Are you offering to whisk me away to strange lands?" There was laughter in his voice.

"And what if I am?"

Calan's expression sobered. "I don't understand. You're teasing me, surely."

Ian stood and walked slowly over to the boy. "No, not this time." He reached out to take Calan's braid in his hand and run it across his palm. Hair had escaped during the course of Calan's work, not surprising given how Calan tended to play with it as he considered one thing or another. The boy's mind and body seemed to always being moving, just like with Ian himself.

We are perfect for each other.

"To be frank, darling boy, I find you irresistible. My desire grows with each encounter between us. It's as if I can't get enough of you."

Calan's breath hitched. "I, um, feel the same way. And I'm ready for you to do whatever you want with me. Past ready, actually."

Those words, said with such naked honesty, caused Ian's guts to tighten—with passion and surprisingly a little fear. In that moment, he knew for a certainty that he wasn't going to offer this boy merely a bit of fun. No, Calan deserved more. "I will not mount you."

"Oh." The disappointment in that one word spoke volumes.

"Not yet. Not today," Ian hurried to qualify. "When I do, it must mean something and do you honor."

"I don't understand."

"Answer my question. Would you truly leave your home, or are you rooted to this place where your only family lives and you're comfortable?"

Calan licked his lips, his gaze shifting from one side to the other. "I love Aunt Celia because she is family and she has taken good care of me. But," he continued with a shrug, "if I spend my whole life in Shadow Valley, I'll always feel as if I've missed out on something."

Relief made Ian's knees weak. He was truly dumbfounded by his own reaction to this boy. Yet, he was a decisive person, and his mind was now made up. "Good." Before Calan could ask for clarification, Ian said, "I'm starving. Someone mentioned something about cheese and tomato sandwiches."

For a moment, he believed Calan wouldn't allow himself to be redirected. Then he nodded. "Okay. Go out and wait in our garden. It's not as impressive as the public ones, but it's too lovely a day to eat inside."

"All right." Ian made himself back away and leave the shed from the same way they'd entered.

To the right was a sweet garden with a wooden table and bench seats. He wandered around to look at all the colorful plants before sitting and leaning his elbows on the worn wood that showed many years of use. Visions of Calan in a kitchen fixing him a meal danced in his head. He liked the idea of being cared for by the boy. It wasn't like the cooks he employed in his manor house. This was more intimate, and while he wanted very much to join Calan and perhaps pin him to a counter to feast on his body instead of sandwiches, he ignored the urge. He'd already pushed the boy with talk of leaving his home. Undoubtedly Calan needed the privacy to mull over what Ian's prodding meant. He should explain to him what he was thinking, except this was a matter of politics and he was duty-bound to raise the issue with those in charge first. It might not be fair to Calan, but it couldn't be helped.

A brown dog with shaggy hair and a tongue lolling wandered into the garden and sniffed at Ian. Apparently satisfied, it sat by his feet, clearly waiting for something. With a chuckle, Ian obliged, scratching the creature behind its ears. This was how he was found when Calan came out of the house carrying a tray. Ian jumped to his feet to take it from him and place it on the table. Calan left and came back out with a pitcher and two cups.

The boy shooed at the dog. "Go home, Benny. None of this is for you." The dog looked mournfully at the table before doing as told and trotting away. Calan started to fill the cups with some kind of cold tea. "That's the neighbor's dog. He somehow always knows when food is being brought out here."

Ian accepted the offered drink and took a healthy swallow. "You don't have a dog of your own?" He welcomed a sandwich that Calan handed him, as well, before sitting down again.

"No. Aunt Celia doesn't believe in pets. I've always wanted one, though." The wistful sound in the boy's voice was heartbreaking. "I suppose you have a lot of dogs for hunting and such."

"I leave the hunting to others, but I do have five dogs simply for the pleasure of their company."

Calan's eyes lit up as he bit into his sandwich. "Five!" he said around his mouthful of food. "How wonderful."

And there will be room for a sixth, if that is what you want. Because it was too tempting to say those words out loud, Ian stuffed his mouth to refrain from doing so. And letch he may be, but Fredric's cheese was delicious. Calan had made enough food for a small army. Ian did it justice, finding himself hungry as if he'd labored hard all day. He would need to get in a good ride before dinner to work off this meal and to gather his thoughts. It would mean leaving Calan for the rest of the afternoon, which would be a hardship. Still, he was a disciplined man, and he had to be strong for the both of them in order to give them what they wanted.

When they were done with the sandwiches, Calan went back into the house and brought back cake. "I baked this in the early morning, so we need to eat it before it gets stale."

Reaching for his slice, he said, "Well then, let me do my part to avoid waste." The sweet was delicious. Calan had a lot of talents, apparently. "I'm afraid I must leave you after this." Calan's crestfallen look nearly made him take back his words. Ian took his hand. "I'm sorry. I must exercise my horse, and I have matters to discuss with my sister." He didn't add that he intended to make his offer to Shadow Valley at the same time. Isabeau could be prudish about certain things, and he wasn't going to leave it solely at her discretion as to whether his plan would be offered to the council members.

"I understand." Calan stood and began to clear the table. "I'll see you at the banquet, though, won't I?"

Ian wrestled the pitcher from Calan's hands as well as the plates and went to the back door. "Of course." He pushed the kitchen door open and entered, not waiting for permission. It was a warm and homey room, ruthlessly clean with everything in proper order. He put everything down on the nearest flat surface and grabbed Calan as he came in behind him.

He had the boy against the counter just as he'd imagined doing earlier and kissed him until his lungs burned for air. Calan panted against him, then squeaked as Ian dropped to his knees and quickly freed the boy's cock. He sucked it down to the root without hesitation, loving the sweet taste of him and desperate to make him come. The moment he swallowed around the shaft, Calan cried out and clutched at Ian's head with sufficient force to make his eyes water. When the boy's shudders had subsided, Ian tucked his dick back into the trousers and stood.

He kissed Calan once more. "That should hold you until tonight."

With a glazed look, the boy nodded. Once Ian was sure Calan could stand without help, he made himself leave, savoring the taste of cum on his tongue and more determined than ever to get his way.

* * * *

Ian timed his return from exercising himself and his horse so that the meeting of the council was nearly done. As he entered the longhouse, he encountered most of his sister's guards roaming the area, alert for danger as they'd been trained to do. They all did a dance around the Shadow Valley people preparing for the evening meal, curious, yet not complacent. He nodded to each one in approval and they did the same to acknowledge his rank. When he reached the door leading to the council chamber, he stopped to rap his knuckles on it in the custom of these people. A moment later, he entered the room, not bothering to wait for an invitation to do so. In his experience, if one asked for something, the answer could always be "no", and he wasn't going to give anyone the chance to stall or thwart his intent before he'd had a chance to make his case.

The female soldier standing behind his sister met him with a stance that indicated she expected trouble. The moment she saw him, however, she relaxed again. As did the Shadow Valley people, their expressions being of only mild surprise and curiosity. Isabeau was different. She frowned at him, a look that had the power to make his belly quiver. This time, though, he was too determined in his goal to give her much mind. Instead, he focused on Fennic.

"Your pardon, sir. I was hoping to speak with the council before the evening meal. If I may be permitted." He gave a shallow and quick bow.

Fennic half rose from his seat, gesturing Ian to come closer. "Of course, my lord. We hadn't realized you were empowered to negotiate on behalf of your king." He flicked his gaze at Isabeau.

"He's not." Isabeau's interjection was issued with a whip-like edge.

Ian hurried to stand beside his sister and put his hand on her shoulder. She all but vibrated with displeasure. "My sister is correct. I am here of my own volition with a newly formed proposal that I believe will benefit both our countries."

Fennic settled back in his chair. "Please proceed, my lord. We are always open to other offers for the treaty. Not that Moorcondia's position thus far has been inadequate," he added with a smile toward Isabeau.

With more than a dozen pair of eyes now trained upon him, Ian felt surprisingly tongue-tied. But he'd spent the entirety of his ride thinking his idea over, looking for any holes in logic or doubts within him. He'd come to this room determined to go through with his plan. Now was not the time to falter, even though if he got his way, his life would be altered forever.

Dropping his hand from his sister's shoulder, he stood with legs braced and hands clasped behind his back—a schoolboy once more giving a presentation to his tutor. "As I've explored your beautiful country, it occurred to me that the most important and successful treaties of my country have been forged with the bonds of matrimony. My sister made that very point, actually, on our journey here." Ignoring the obvious stiffening of Isabeau's body, he plunged on. "I would like to propose the same path be taken for this one between Moorcondia and Shadow Valley."

There was a stunned silence, which was better than an all-out screeching of dissent. Then, with furrowed brows, Fennic asked, "Are you suggesting that Lady Isabeau marry one of…us?"

Ian knew of only one man on the council who was unattached, and the look on the man's face was one of delightful surprise. Ian couldn't see his sister's expression, but he didn't have to. He needed to clear up the mistaken impression immediately.

"Not at all, sir. I would never speak for my sister, and I know she grieves still for her late husband. In any event, my idea involves myself." He kept his gaze trained on Fennic and not Celia. That woman was too shrewd not to understand his meaning already. He took a bracing breath before continuing. "My offer involves my marriage to Calan."

Audible gasps reverberated around the room, Fennic's included. The man recovered his shock quickly, however. "Are we to understand that you are offering to marry Councilwoman Celia's nephew? As in take him as your wife?" Now the man's eyebrows all but disappeared in his hairline.

Isabeau stood abruptly. "I would speak with you in private, brother."

Ian kept his eyes on Fennic. "Yes, sir. That is exactly what I'm proposing. I have become quite fond of him in our short acquaintance, and as you know, men marrying each other is acceptable under Moorcondian law." Now, he turned to Isabeau, ignoring how fire practically shot out of the top of her head. "It has become a valuable and effective part of our diplomacy, as my sister can attest."

He tried to convey how important this was to him by staring at Isabeau with a kind of intensity he'd used their whole lives. As cavalier as he could be with many things, they'd long ago developed a wordless way of confirming when he was being serious. His sister's narrowing gaze conveyed her displeasure, but she sat again and curtly nodded once.

Ian looked at all the council members with a quick sweep, forcing himself to focus on Celia for a few seconds more than the others. This woman was not the final say with the council, but it was her nephew he was making an offer for. And while he didn't know much about Shadow Valley's laws, he had to assume that a relative's opinion weighed heavily in the decision-making. He tried to convey reassurance over his sincerity.

Fennic scratched his chin. "I don't think our laws say anything about it one way or the other. The issue hasn't come up before, has it?" he asked the room in general. There was general murmuring among the crowd, although thankfully there didn't appear to be any hostilities over the matter.

Unless one counted Celia. The woman rose to a stand. "It's of no importance whether our law specifically disallows it. The idea is absurd on the face of it. Two men may...*enjoy* each other's company. That is not to say that our custom acknowledges a formal marriage between the two. That bond is for establishing families — creating a new generation so that our people survive."

Silence followed that pronouncement, and Ian felt his heart sink. He'd been so sure that the Shadow Valley people wouldn't object to his proposal.

Then another woman slowly stood. "I don't deny that your view of marriage's role in our society is correct, but are you saying that because my dear husband and I have been unable to have children that our marriage does not count?" The look of sorrow on the woman's face was the epitome of pain. Clearly, being childless had been an unhappy fate.

"Certainly not," Celia was quick to reply. "It's only that… Surely this council isn't considering sacrificing my nephew for the sake of successful diplomacy. That isn't fair to Calan. Everyone in Shadow Valley has agency when it comes to their future. Are we going to toss aside generations of customs and rules merely for the sake of a treaty that we don't even need." She glared in a way that encompassed Ian and Isabeau alike.

Ian's hackles went up. He hadn't intended to interfere with his sister's mission…not much, anyway. And not so as to jeopardize it. What he offered was an extra benefit to the treaty effort. It wasn't supposed to be seen as some kind of negative.

"I take your point, madam, but while I'll leave it to Lady Isabeau to enumerate the many benefits of the treaty, I can assure you that I have no intention of forcing Calan into anything." He turned his attention back to Fennic. "I expect that if the council approves of the union, it will ultimately be up to the boy to agree to it."

Fennic nodded. "Just so. We would never force him. And there is great value in what you suggest." The man focused his gaze on Celia. "The one sticking point in particular in our negotiations has been the disposition of your recent cordial. Keeping it in the family with a marriage of Calan to the count would be an elegant solution to the problem, don't you agree?"

Before the woman could respond, Ian jumped in. "If that is of concern, I can assure you that although I'm not related to the king, my status as a count puts me at the second tier of the nobility. I have the power to control specific items of commerce, as would my wife by extension. If Calan has dominion over the distribution of this cordial within Moorcondia, would that make a difference in your acceptance of a treaty?" He could tell by the shifting emotions in the room that he'd hit upon the solution.

"Except he wouldn't have the power, would he?" Celia spat out. "As his husband, you would control what he does."

Ian tried for a conciliatory smile, although he believed that there was nothing he could say to sway the woman. It wasn't at all clear that her resistance to the plan was based on a real concern for Calan. Rather, he sensed that it was her own power that she worried about. "While it is true that my word is law within my own county, I'm not a tyrant to anyone, least of all with my own wife. I will treat him with the utmost respect and…tenderness."

He meant what he said, although the visions in his head about what he'd do to the boy in bed were passionate to the point of ferocity. He had to work to keep his thoughts off his face and out of his dick. There was more to say to convince the council. "And wives in Moorcondia own and manage their own property. Calan would be no different. Such right can be written into the treaty, as well, can it not, sister?" He shot Isabeau the winningest smile that he could.

Isabeau grimaced. "*Yes*." The tightness in her voice warned him that whatever happened in this room, she had a *lot* to say to him.

Fennic raised his hands. "Well, it seems as if we have a new path forward — with Calan's agreement, of course. Shall we adjourn for dinner and return to this topic tomorrow after we have his answer?"

And with that, Ian had to hide a victorious smile. He had no doubt that the boy would agree. The attraction between them couldn't be ignored, and if what little they'd shared to date foretold what their lives would be like with each other, this marriage would suit them both very well indeed.

* * * *

Calan hurried downstairs, smoothing his tunic and patting his braid. He'd spent too long in the workshop, trying to be productive, yet distracted by thoughts of Ian. It had been disappointing when the man had left after lunch, but the time apart had probably been a good idea. The man's proximity clouded Calan's mind and overtook control of his body. At least alone, he'd been able to ponder what he truly wanted, and there was no doubt in his mind that he wanted Ian to take him fully as a lover. The promise of a future mounting had firmed his desire for the count, and although disappointed in the slowness of their relationship, he also liked the idea of the man being careful with him. Ian's measured approach to their relationship showed respect. He did not think of Calan as a quick release for his passion. And his mastery of the situation that normally would have irked Calan's sense of independence for some reason didn't. There was comfort in knowing someone he liked and trusted was taking care of him.

As he reached the living area, the front door flew open. Celia's face was twisted in fury. Before Calan could issue an apology for something he didn't understand he'd done, the woman marched over and slapped him. The sting was more to his pride than his cheek, and sadly he was used to the corporal punishment. He stood blinking back tears, trying to think of what he'd done to earn such ire.

"You slut! Was it your plan all along to have him take you away from me?"

"W-what?" He was having trouble understanding what she was saying. *Does Ian want to take me with him?* The idea of being the man's lover for longer than a few days elated him. His aunt's answer caused his heart to skip.

"Don't play innocent with me. He's proposed to marry you to bind the treaty. The entire council is overjoyed at the idea, although his sister isn't as keen." She shifted her gaze over his shoulder. "That's something, anyway."

"I don't understand, Aunt Celia. How can that happen?"

She narrowed her gaze, fury written across her face. "The Moorcondians think themselves above any convention. Men taking boy brides has become common among them, apparently. Ridiculous!" Throwing up her hands, she circled the room before coming back to him. "Fennic has agreed that it must be your choice. You will refuse the offer when it's made tonight after the banquet."

Calan was still stunned at the news. "I will?"

Celia raised her hand again, then let it drop before it landed on his face. "*Yes*, you ungrateful boy. Some day you will light my funeral pyre and can do what you like. Until then, you will do as you're told."

Calan had always been grateful for his aunt's care and obedient even when he disagreed with her. It seemed little enough, given how much he owed her. This demand, however, made his heart ache. It wasn't merely that he longed to lose his virginity to Ian. There was something more lurking within him that caused him grief at the idea of rebuffing the man.

He was a dutiful nephew, though, and gave the only accepting answer. "Yes, ma'am." He lowered his gaze, not so much to be contrite as to hide the resentment he felt.

"Good. I'll be but a moment to change, then we will go. This ridiculous notion of a marriage can be dealt with and perhaps the whole treaty will fall apart. That would be the best outcome, and perhaps I'll owe the count a debt of gratitude for doing what I've been unable to thus far."

Calan stood in the same spot, waiting with as much patience as he'd ever had. Outwardly, he was calm and complacent. Inside him there raged a storm of confusion and unhappiness. Traveling had always been nothing but a dream, and living elsewhere for the rest of his life hadn't featured in it. Shadow Valley was the home he loved, and while visiting new places appealed to him, what Ian was proposing meant a permanent move from his homeland. He might never see it again, and what did it mean to be Ian's wife? There would be mounting, of course — probably a great deal of it. That thought spread warmth through him, forcing him to control his cock's effort to harden. But there was more to marriage than sex. Would he become chatelaine of Ian's household, directing servants and planning banquets? He had no experience with such matters. There was no way he could please Ian in that way. And what if the man tired of him in bed? Powerful men often took lovers outside of marriage, didn't they? He rubbed the spot over his heart at the idea he'd be expected to share the man.

"Come now." Celia straightened the cuffs of her formal dress as she strode toward the door.

Calan followed as he always did, silent. This time, though, his mind was whirl of thoughts and feelings, conflicting and confusing. He barely noticed the journey to the longhouse until they were entering the large room and the din of many people inside it. He kept his gaze downward as he made his way to his assigned seat. Ian's presence could be felt somehow, and Calan knew where to find him if he looked. He dared not. His misery would surely be noticed by the man, and there was no point in making them both unhappy while they ate. Not that Calan had the stomach for food… He picked at his plate and was both relieved and alarmed when the meal ended.

Calan tried not to drag his feet when Fennic called for him to come to the council room. He'd never seen it before, yet lacked any interest is taking in his surroundings. The heat of Ian's gaze was impossible to ignore now that they were enclosed in a smaller space. Looking up, the count's face was right in his line of vision. He saw concern there, but also more— encouragement. Ian shot a brief smile at him before taking his seat next to his sister. Everyone was doing the same, and Calan realized Fennic was gesturing him toward a chair between him and Celia. Calan took it, careful not to look at his aunt. She was no doubt delighted to thwart the plans of everyone there, especially the Moorcondians.

Fennic put his hand on Calan's arm. "My dear boy, I expect your aunt has apprised you of the count's offer of marriage to seal the treaty."

Calan nodded and swallowed past a painful lump in his throat. "Yes, sir."

Fennic patted him a few times. "Good. And I'm sure you also understand that we would never make such a decision for you. No desire for a treaty can override our customs. No one in Shadow Valley is forced into a marriage not of their choosing. So, we ask you now — do you accept the count's proposal?"

It were as if time stopped, no one moving, nothing stirring. All Calan could hear was the pounding of his own heart and the rushing of blood through his veins. For a few moments, he didn't even breathe until his head swam from lack of air. He clenched his hands in his lap to ground his tension and keep his expression neutral. *You know what to say.* There really was no choice, except he couldn't resist the urge to raise his gaze and look right at Ian. What he saw there chased all doubt away and governed his tongue before he even realized what was happening.

"Yes."

Chapter Six

Ian hefted the heavy basket higher onto his arm. "Are you sure about all of this, Isabeau? I mean salt, flour, cheese, honey and wine as gifts to the bride's family don't seem very ingratiating."

"Yes, I am."

He didn't need to see his sister's face to know she was still seething over what he'd done and the outcome of his offer. She'd unleashed her cutting tongue on him after the council meeting, but since Calan's acceptance, she'd stopped talking about it. Her silent disapproval was equally harsh. But as the marriage had broken through problems in the negotiation of the treaty and had led to it being almost ready to sign that very morning, the deal was as done as it needed to be as far as he was concerned. She'd successfully fulfilled the task their king had given her. The man would be pleased, and the court would rightfully fete her upon their return. And however she felt, she was at least performing the Shadow Valley customs as the sum total of the groom's family.

Ian flicked his gaze down at the animal she led on a leash. "And the goat, too?" He knew he was being stupid about all of it. His sister would have been meticulous in determining the various details of what was expected of them. It was hard to follow the formalities, though, when all he wanted was to get Calan wedded and bedded.

"Yes," Isabeau bit out. "Not that it had to be a goat, per se," she added. "Any farm animal would have done. This happened to be the easiest one to procure. You'll pay me back what I paid for it, of course."

"Of course." Ian knew his sister would never come calling for the payment. She was simply giving an outlet to her anger. The afternoon was doomed to be very uncomfortable for them both.

Calan's aunt was duty-bound to welcome them into her home. That didn't mean she wasn't going to make it as unpleasant as possible. The look on the woman's face when Calan had accepted the proposal had been frightening. Her fury had been a palpable thing, sufficient to make Ian worried for Calan's safety. Yet, when he'd tried to speak with the boy, it had been Fennic who'd stopped him. Apparently, the betrothed couple had to be separated until the groom had paid homage to the bride's family and been welcomed into their home with some kind of ceremony involving tea, of all things.

"What exactly is supposed to happen?"

Isabeau shrugged. "I have no idea. I didn't ask because it's not up to us to do anything, and beyond our duties, I don't—"

"Care. You've made your feelings on this matter very clear." It was disheartening, but he also knew his sister and believed she would come around in the end.

"You can't be surprised by this. I've made my feelings on the matter of marrying a woman and producing heirs very clear." He stopped and waited until Isabeau stopped as well. "I have no interest in bedding women, as you well know. Calan..." He sighed. "I want him very much and if I can satisfy my own desires and do some good for my king and country, then why not?"

"I didn't need your help, you know. The treaty was close to being finalized. I would have found a path forward on my own."

"Of that, I have no doubt. This wasn't meant to reflect badly on you, sister. It's merely a matter of my giving into my urges without dishonoring Calan. Helping the negotiations is merely a side benefit."

Isabeau looked away from him. "Then you must lie in this bed you made, and the gods help you." With that, she started on her way with determined steps.

Ian caught up with her and nearly stumbled as they rounded a corner and Celia's house came into view. The woman stood in front of it, but it was not the sight of her that grabbed him by the balls and squeezed the breath out of him. Calan was to the side and one step behind his aunt. He was dressed in a loose tunic and trousers in buttercup yellow. His lovely hair cascaded over his shoulders, save for a skinny braid at each temple. Dainty flowers that matched the color of his clothing were entwined within the strands. As Ian and Isabeau approached, the boy smiled shyly.

Ian positioned his heavy basket to hide his burgeoning erection and willed himself under control. Whatever occurred during this visit, he would endure with good cheer, no matter how tedious or irritating it was. His patience would be rewarded soon enough with this fetching boy in his bed and in his life forever.

If the permanency of his plans for Calan should have been alarming after such a long time of bachelorhood, he was happy to discover that wasn't the case. Getting married held an appeal for him now that he wouldn't have expected. *Because it's with the right person.* Such a simple explanation—and yet one that had never occurred to him before Calan had come into his life.

He let Isabeau take the lead. Stopping in front of Celia, she inclined her head briefly before holding out the leash. "Thank you for inviting us to your home. On behalf of the Charteris family, I present to you this gift."

For a few tense moments, Celia didn't respond. Then she also inclined her head. "Welcome to my home." She gestured toward Calan. "Take it out back."

Calan didn't hesitate to do as he'd been told. The boy dared to flash a grin at Ian before leading the goat around to the back of the house. He smiled in return. Isabeau cleared her throat and shot him a look that broke the spell of watching Calan.

Stepping forward, Ian held out his basket. "Please accept these items as a show of my devotion to your nephew."

Celia liberated the basket from his grasp, showing no indication that it was heavy or that the offerings were appreciated. Instead, she turned and took the few steps necessary to open her front door. She held it for them. "Please enter. I hope my meager hospitality honors you." Those words were probably always said as part of the custom, because he doubted very much she actually meant any of it. Her tone implied as much, but there was no point in dwelling on *that*.

He and Isabeau entered the small house. It was clean and organized, not exactly cozy. Indeed, with Isabeau and Celia inside all but squaring off, there was a distinct chill in the air. That all evaporated when Calan came through from the kitchen. His beautiful face lit up the room. Ian figured he could stand anything so long as he could stare at the boy.

Celia shoved the basket at her nephew. "Calan, bring the kettle. We'll get started now."

The boy turned on his heel with his burden and went back the way he'd come while Celia led Ian and Isabeau over to a couch and two chairs by the fireplace. Warm as the weather was, there was no fire burning, leaving the spot a bit gloomy because it was far from the windows. The Shadow Valley woman indicated that he and his sister should take the chairs. Celia perched herself on the edge of the couch. A low table sat between them, laden with delicate sandwiches and pastries, as well as cups and saucers. It was obvious that this was their tableware reserved for special occasions.

When Calan returned, he hefted a large copper kettle by its handle. Ian started to rise to help him, but Celia's stern gaze had him sitting again. As hard as it was to acquiesce, he understood that he had to play this out by the terms of his host. Once Calan was his, however, the boy would be pampered. Ian would make it his life's work.

Calan placed the kettle on an iron trivet that swung out from the fireplace on a long arm that reached the end of the table. Then the boy sat next to his aunt and went about making tea, except it was all done with slow, stylized movements that highlighted the solemnity of the occasion. There was a grace to it all, no matter how tedious it proved to be for a man like Ian. He focused on Calan's fine hands and the way his hair swayed as he moved. Not surprisingly, it all became fascinating simply by virtue of the fact that it was Calan doing it. *How has this boy managed to get under my skin so quicky and into my...heart?* No, that was too fanciful a thought. He shoved it aside and focused only on what was happening before him. When Calan held out the first cup of tea to him, Ian took it carefully and sipped.

He had no idea what the expected thing to say was, but he didn't have to think about it. He spoke sincerely to Calan only. "Perfect." The blush that bloomed on Calan's fair cheeks told him he had hit his mark.

"I am honored to please you." Calan lowered his eyes and peeked up at him from under his lashes in that slightly naughty way he had.

Everything in Ian tightened, his balls most of all, and his dick strained against its confines. It had never entirely softened, and now it made him desperate to find a secluded place with Calan. There was no chance of that. So, he gazed at his cup of tea as if it held the secrets of the world and waited patiently as Calan served first Isabeau, then Celia and finally himself. There was drinking and eating and chatter, mostly between the women. It was all stilted but also mercifully rushed. None of them wanted to be there any longer than necessary.

Finally, Celia put down her empty cup and spoke to Calan. "You may dally with your betrothed in the garden while Lady Isabeau and I clean up."

There was a moment's hesitation before Ian shot to his feet. "How kind of you, madam. Sister," he added with a beseeching nod to Isabeau. He doubted she'd ever so much as rinsed a cup in her life. Certainly she hadn't been raised to and had a veritable army of servants at Truehart Manor.

Being the lady that she was, Isabeau smiled serenely and acted as if she did dishes routinely. "Of course, I'm happy to be of assistance."

Relieved, Ian held out his hand to Calan. When the boy clasped it, Ian tugged him out of the room with perhaps more haste than was polite. But whatever hope he'd had of getting hold of more of the boy, they were dashed once they were outside. Calan pulled free and put a few steps between them.

"I know what you want, my lord, but it shall have to wait until after we are married."

If it had a mouth, his cock would have howled. He took a step closer. "Why is that? We've already shared...intimacies. I only want a kiss." He made a playful grab for the boy.

Calan danced away and headed toward the far side of the yard where the goat stood tied to a post and munching on grass. "Those are the rules. No one would have cared if you'd fucked me when we were merely lovers, as long as we'd been discreet. Now that we are engaged, decorum must be maintained, and everyone is watching us, whether we know it or not."

Ian rearranged himself, and he sauntered over to join the boy. "That doesn't make any sense."

Calan shrugged. "You should have looked into it before asking for my hand in marriage. I could have told you, for example." Folding his arms, the boy glared at him. Gone was the coyness.

"Ah." Ian clasped his hands behind him. "You're irked that I went to the council first. In my defense, I did sound you out about leaving Shadow Valley, and given the politics involved, I decided it was necessary to float the idea with the powers that be before asking you. If it makes you feel better, my sister is livid with me for similar reasons."

Calan's expression softened, and he dropped his arms. "I'm not angry, not really. It was just…a surprise, that's all. My aunt isn't exactly happy with me, either."

Ian wanted to wrap the boy up in his arms to comfort him yet dared not. Touching Calan would be too hard a test of his self-control. "I trust she hasn't been making life too difficult for you."

By way of an answer, Calan merely shrugged. He gestured toward the goat. "This was a very nice wedding gift."

Ian was willing to change the subject if that was what his betrothed wanted. Their wedding would happen within a couple of days' time, at which point, Celia would lose her power over her nephew, and Ian could protect him. "Is it? I'm glad. Isabeau handled all of that." He looked around the yard. He hadn't seen any other farm animals. "What will your aunt do with it?"

Calan looked surprised. "Oh, it's going to be the main meal at our wedding feast."

"Oh yes? Goat will be a first for me. I'm sure I'll love it."

Calan cocked his head. "You really don't know anything about what you're getting yourself into, do you?"

"Not when it comes to the 'before the wedding' part." He wished that he'd bothered to ask some questions. If he had, he'd have made sure that Isabeau procured a pig instead. Pork had to be far tastier than goat, in his estimation. No matter. Calan seemed genuinely pleased, and that's what counted. "I promise

I excel at the after-wedding customs." He let his meaning show through his gaze.

On cue, Calan blushed again. "I have no doubt, my lord. You could have had all of that without the lifelong commitment."

Ian got serious because it was important that Calan understood his feelings on the matter. "I know. You've been very generous with yourself, but I am a greedy man. I want all of you all the time."

"Oh, well. It's a good thing I feel the same way. But we both have to wait a couple of more days. Those are the rules, my lord, and perhaps it's because I've broken quite a few of them in my life, I find I really want to obey these."

"And so we shall." Ian took one more step closer and leaned in. "You are worth the wait, darling boy."

* * * *

It was funny how two days could feel like a lifetime when one was waiting for something they truly desired. Ian had dug deep for patience during the Shadow Valley's betrothal customs. The welcoming tea ceremony at Councilwoman Celia's house had been followed the next day by a gathering at the longhouse of the council and friends hosted by Isabeau and Amalie. As his only relatives available, the task had fallen to them to reciprocate on behalf of the groom's family, despite the gifts they'd given already. At least the party had been more lively, with music and a large meal of local delicacies. But, as with the previous event, Ian and Calan were not afforded any real opportunity to be together. Everyone acted as chaperones, guarding the bride's virtue in an old-fashioned way that had mostly fallen out of favor in Moorcondia. Not so much, apparently, in Shadow Valley. The forced celibacy had been driving Ian mad. His only outlet for his constant state of arousal had been his own hand, and that was wholly inadequate, given Calan's proximity.

It all changes tonight.

The wedding was now finally upon them. Calan had chosen to have the ceremony by the fountain at the heart of the maze. It was the bride's prerogative to choose the place for the wedding, and with the agreeable weather, this outdoor venue suited it very well. As Ian stood in his black velvet tunic and trousers trimmed with gold, he was glad that he'd brought formal clothing on the chance that Shadow Valley would require it for some occasion. He wanted to look his best when he bound himself to his bride. It was a matter of pride, and Calan deserved the best that Ian could give him. He had no idea what the boy, himself, would be wearing, but it hardly mattered. He was always stunning in Ian's eyes.

Beside him, his sister and niece were beautifully decked out in matching blue silk gowns with seed pearls sewn into the bodices. Amalie was practically vibrating with excitement. Unlike her mother, the girl had no trouble accepting the idea of Ian marrying another man. She was thrilled to be a part of it all, however minor her role. Given how young she was, she probably didn't appreciate that this union guaranteed that she would one day be the Countess of Charteris. Ian was pleased with that outcome. It freed him to enjoy his marriage without guilt, and while Isabeau's silent censure was a disappointment, he also hoped she'd come around to accepting Calan as Ian's wife.

A sudden hush among the milling crowd told him his bride had arrived. A moment later, the guests parted and Calan came into view. He was on his aunt's arm, but Ian barely noticed the dour woman. His gaze was homed in on the boy, resplendent in all white. His long tunic flowed out by his calves, and his trousers were gathered at his ankles. Cloth shoes the color of oatmeal blended into the packed earth path, giving the impression that he floated above the ground. A garland of colorful flowers served as a belt, and a small version of the same sat on his head like a crown. In his hand, Calan clutched a sprig of white and lavender flowers. There was nothing to read in his expression, closed-off as it was and solemn. Ian knew a moment of worry that perhaps now that the time was upon him, Calan was having second thoughts. His heart lightened in the next instant when Calan winked at him. The boldness of his wife-to-be delighted him. He wanted to break out in a broad grin, but the moment his lips twitched, Isabeau elbowed him in his side. Taking the hint, he set a serious expression on his face.

Celia led Calan in a slow circle around Ian and his family three times, showing him to everyone gathered, before stopping in front of him. With a look that could curdle milk, the councilwoman offered Calan's right hand. Ian understood what to do. He clasped the boy with his left hand and gave it a brief squeeze of encouragement. Then he turned them both to face the officiant, the oldest person on the council. The woman had long, gray hair and a comforting smile. She clearly had no trouble with the marriage. The tension Ian felt in Calan eased as the woman tied a long white cord around their wrists to hold them together. Then it was all about the vows. Ian heard the woman's words, spoke those required of him, but his concentration was focused fully on his bride — the bowing of his head, the movement of his soft, pink lips, the serious tone of his answers to the officiant's questions. Each moment brought the boy closer to being his.

There was one awkward moment toward the end when each of their family representatives was asked if she accepted the vows of the couple as true and right. After a fraught hesitation, Celia bit out the proper response. Isabeau was far better at doing her duty as expected, but knowing her as he did, Ian heard the lack of sincerity in her tone. Calan showed his distress with a tightening of his fingers clenched around Ian's. He squeezed back, rubbing his thumb along the boy's finger to soothe him. It worked. Calan once more relaxed in his grip and smiled broadly when the officiant pronounced that they were married. Ian gave into his growing temptation to kiss the boy, lifting him in his free arm and melding their lips together. He wanted to take it longer and deeper, yet knew it wouldn't be proper and with their wrists still bound, it was awkward. So, he contented himself with the brief contact and allowed the crowd to sweep them away.

The celebration meal was being held in the longhouse. Unlike for the other banquets, the tables were configured differently. One was stationed at the far end of the room horizontally, set with only five places. This was for the happy couple and their family. The others were formed in vertical rows across the room for the guests, of which there were many. Ian figured it was the entire village...or close to it. Everyone was in a jovial mood. Once Ian and Calan were stationed by their seats, Celia came up to hand Ian a short, plain dagger. Because she held it out hilt first,

Ian was not alarmed, but he wasn't sure what he was supposed to do other than accept it with a nod of thanks.

"It's to cut the cord binding us," Calan leaned in to whisper.

"Ah." Ian obliged, careful not to nick his bride's soft skin.

Calan caught the cord before it fell and deftly wound it around the flowers he still clutched. "It symbolizes how you are going to take my virginity, although I'm not sure if many brides are still virgins when they marry. *I* am, as you well know."

Ian nearly choked on his spit. "I really should have paid more attention to Isabeau when she was schooling me about your marriage customs." With a grin, he held out Calan's seat for him.

The meal was sumptuous by Shadow Valley standards, with wine flowing freely and everyone chattering and laughing with obvious enjoyment. The unfortunate goat—which proved to be more tender and not as gamey as he'd expected—was reserved for the bridal party only. Isabeau was paying for it all, and she was nothing if not an excellent hostess when it came to parties. She even seemed to loosen up herself over the affair, and Amalie was beyond happy to be included in such adult activities. She wasn't the only child, either. The ceremony had occurred in the late afternoon, so no one other than the very young were staying up past their bedtime. Ian thought it quite civilized to conduct marriages at the end of the day instead of the morning. Once the banquet was over, he would have Calan all to himself for the entire night and into the next day as much as he liked. *That* part he *had* been paying attention to.

As the meal was coming to an end, musicians arrived and started playing. Calan tapped Ian's arm. "We are expected to dance."

"We are?" More information he'd glossed over, yet except for delaying their leave-taking, he didn't mind. Dancing was something he did enjoy.

Taking Calan's hand, he led his bride to the floor in front of the musicians and gently tugged Calan into his arms. If there was some local dance he was supposed to follow, he had no knowledge of it, so he simply led the boy in a slow circle as he would have back home. He held their bodies flush against one another. This close, his arousal was obvious and more importantly, he could feel Calan's in response.

He leaned in to whisper for Calan's ears only. "What you do to me, *wife*." The sound of himself saying that word sent a frisson of excitement down his spine. He liked how possessive it made him feel — and protective. Whatever Calan's life had been up until now, Ian was going to make it his constant duty to give him the best of everything. And he would be safe with him. Celia's disapproving face came into view. Ian stared back at her, trying to convey with his eyes alone that her reign over the boy was done. She couldn't hurt him anymore, something he was certain she'd done many times in the past.

Calan ran his fingers along Ian's shoulder, catching his attention once more. "Is it bad for me to want this all to be over quickly? I think you can tell I want you as urgently as you do me."

Ian smiled. "It is very wicked, indeed, for you to wish to leave our guests so soon. And, as your husband…I approve. How much longer do we need to linger to observe the expected proprieties?"

Calan gnawed at his lower lip. "There will be more dancing, with the guests joining in. Then there's cake…"

"Well, cake is always worth waiting for, just so long as you leave room for me to fill you up, too."

Calan gasped and popped his eyes. "My lord, what kind of randy talk is that? Do it some more," he added with a fluttering of his lashes.

Ian was happy to oblige.

* * * *

Ian was not so lust-driven that he couldn't appreciate how his assigned quarters had been decked out in a romantic way. The room was filled with flowers of various kinds, and red rose petals had been strewn across the bed. The bedding, including the canopy, had been replaced, as well. Gone were the muted brown ones, replaced by sparkling white. The contrast between the comforter and the petals was stark—and not very subtle. It was based on the primitive notion that a bride was going to be shed of her virginity with the spilling of some blood. While Calan's purity was not in question, the boy would only bleed if Ian let his lust overtake his caution. That was not going to happen, even though his cock strained and ached with the need to fill his bride's ass. He was a master of control, and that mattered more now than it ever had before.

"It's all so beautiful." Calan looked at him with pure joy. "I never expected to have a bridal room in my life. Thank you."

"As much as I love your appreciation, I can't claim credit for any of this." Ian closed the gap between them and gave his bride a chaste kiss. At Calan's whimper of disappointment, Ian chuckled. "I dare not do more at this point. Your clothing is lovely, and I wouldn't want it to be ruined by my need to get my hands on you."

Calan's entire face, and even his neck, pinked up, a typical reaction that Ian adored. "I feel equally enthusiastic, my lord. Let me tend to my disrobement myself...and quickly." The boy did not waste time, although the first thing he did was tie his wedding bouquet upside-down to a drawer handle. "It's to dry it out so that I can preserve it." He wrinkled his nose. "I'm supposed to keep it in our bedroom to promote fertility. It's silly in my case, obviously."

Sensing an underlying concern, Ian felt obligated to respond. "I think that's a sweet tradition, one that I would love for you to observe. It doesn't matter that we can never have children. Don't ever worry on that account. Amalie will make a great countess when the time comes, and I am more content with that result."

"I know, and I can't say I'm disappointed myself about not fathering children. I do better with animals than people." He carefully undid his sash and laid it on the chest of drawers. "I can get a dog of my own though, right?"

"As many as you want, my dear."

"That's all I want, then. Well, not all..." he added as he stripped off his shoes. Then came his trousers and finally he lifted his tunic over his head, revealing his slender, hard cock jutting out from his groin. He stood tall and unabashed. "I'm ready for you. I mean really ready. My channel is coated with a cream that will make the passage of your cock easy. There's more over on the nightstand."

Ian didn't shift his gaze, mesmerized by the sight of his bride and the words of how eager the boy had been for this moment. He wouldn't have thought anything could make him want Calan more. He'd have been wrong, and with a silent apology to his tailor, he ripped his clothes off.

Chapter Seven

Calan quivered with anticipation as he watched his husband's clothes fly away. It was hard to wrap his mind around the idea that he was now married and would soon be leaving his home in Shadow Valley for a new one in Moorcondia. He worried he wouldn't be able to make the transition well and that his life would be curtailed in ways that even his aunt hadn't imposed. But those high-level considerations aside, the one thing he knew for certainty was that he was ready to be bedded by this man. He was glad that his earlier efforts to get a lover had failed. It was right and proper that his innocence was Ian's to take. His well-lubricated hole clenched at the sight of the man's long, thick cock. But this was nothing new. He'd seen Ian naked before and so wasn't surprised by what was coming. Ian would be careful and better yet, make it good for him. There was no doubt of that in Calan's mind. He wasn't going to hesitate giving himself completely to this man.

When Ian stalked over to him. Calan braced for a passionate embrace. Instead, he got a slew of chaste kisses along his lips and jawline while his husband ran his fingers lightly down Calan's arms. His skin got goosebumps from the touch, and he shivered. When their hard dicks bumped, he gasped and leaned into Ian for more contact. His effort was thwarted by Ian picking him up and cradling him in his strong arms, as if Calan weighed nothing more than his wedding bouquet. There was more kissing along the way, but nothing as passionate as Calan longed for. Ian managed to tear back the comforter and put one knee on the side of the bed and lay Calan in the middle on the cool sheets. Calan grasped hold of the man's arms, determined to keep him close. He needn't have worried. His husband followed him down and covered his body with his own.

Ian's weight was nearly crushing, but Calan didn't mind. He liked the feeling of being mastered by this man. And the position allowed their cocks to slip and slide along each other. Sparks of pleasure made him groan and arch into Ian's embrace. He undulated his hips to increase the friction. The simple contact threatened to make him come. That was fine by him. Calan had no doubt that this night would bring many orgasms. One little one at the beginning would help take the edge off.

His husband had other ideas, however. Lifting off him, Ian held Calan flush against the bedding by holding his shoulders down. He straddled Calan by his waist, keeping their dicks apart. When Calan tried to buck up, the maddening man clamped his knees against Calan's sides, anchoring him more to the spot. Trapped, he could only frown and moan out his frustration. Ian's low chuckle floated over him. And the kissing continued, traveling along his jaw and over to his earlobe. Ian took it in his teeth and scraped along the soft tissue. Calan gasped at the unexpected pleasure that small aggression gave him. His cock jerked, and his hole spasmed.

"So responsive. So eager." Ian licked and nipped along Calan's collarbone. "I love that about you."

The sound of that loaded word—love—made Calan's heart stutter. He put it aside, knowing that in the throes of passion, it didn't mean anything. His husband simply enjoyed having an eager bed mate to mount. If that, plus companionship, was the most they would get out of their marriage, it would be enough. A small voice in the back of his head disagreed. He ignored it and focused on the ripples of pleasure coursing through his body as Ian made his way to his bobbing dick. The man nuzzled it first, with small touches and soft rubbing that nevertheless drove Calan wild. Then Ian licked a stripe from base to cockhead, tickling the bundle of nerves under it, before swallowing the shaft whole.

Calan arched into his husband's mouth. "Oh, Ian! Yes, please, more of that."

There was another chuckle, this time along Calan's shaft. He felt the vibrations down to his balls. He grabbed hold of his husband's head and clutched at his hair. When the man slid his hand between Calan's thighs and pressed a finger past his hole, he cried out. Ian swallowed around his cock and that, in combination with how the finger dragged across his sensitive spot, sent Calan spiraling into a climax. He shimmied and clenched both his hole and his own fingers around the sheet, keeping the man inside from leaving him and shoving his dick as far down Ian's throat as possible.

Ian stayed with him until the last shudders eased. Of course, he did. The man was a wonderful and generous lover. He worked Calan's shaft with his tongue as he pulled off it, but he kept his finger pressed deep inside his ass, thrusting slowly. For long seconds, Calan couldn't do more than lie there, panting and with his arms spread out. He continued to let his husband do as he wanted. *I'm his to play with however he wants.* He didn't resist when Ian used first one knee, then the other, to spread Calan's legs wide. Calan raised his heels without being asked, to plant the sole of each foot flat on the bed and give his husband better access to his ass.

"You are so clever—and brave and beautiful," Ian whispered, his voice thick. "I won't last long once I'm inside you."

Thrilled at the notion that he had such a strong effect on the man, Calan gave a lazy smile and opened his eyes. The intensity he saw shining through Ian's as he stared back at him made him bold. Squeezing his hole as tightly as he could to capture the man's finger, he said, "I won't mind. We have all night. Please mount me, husband."

Ian bared his teeth and moaned. In that glorious moment, he seemed to be reduced to being an animal, one determined to claim his mate. He pulled out his finger, a potential disappointment, except it was apparently only so that he could reach over to grab the pot of cream. With his gaze re-fixed on Calan, Ian slathered the lubricant over his cock.

Ian pushed the back of Calan's legs to expose him even more before sliding closer to his ass. "I will take this slow, my dear." His voice conveyed how much strain he was under.

"I don't want that." To emphasize his point, Calan clasped his own knees and pulled his legs as close to his shoulders as he could get, bowing his body and freeing Ian's hands for better use.

Calan forced his eyes to stay open so that he could see his husband's face as that massive cock pressed against Calan's hole. The breech made his breath catch — the way it stretched him wider than any fingers had ever done. But instead of pulling away, Calan pushed out with his sphincter muscles, something he'd heard could make it easier for Ian's cock to get in deeper. The man's nostrils flared, and he slid his hands under Calan's ass in order to cradle his hips. With that as leverage, Ian slid his cock farther and farther until his large balls smacked against Calan's backside. The feeling of fullness was both strange and wonderous. This was what it meant to be conquered by one's husband. Calan closed his eyes and savored the way the man's cock pressed against the soft tissue of his channel. When Ian remained still, Calan gripped the shaft with deliberate spasms in silent invitation to fuck him.

Being a clever man, Ian understood. He began to thrust, slowly at first, but something inside Calan's ass snapped. That which had been tight, loosened, giving his husband easy access. With the vague discomfort of being stuffed dissipating, Calan relaxed into the sensations of that marvelous dick rubbing his prostate. His dick hardened, and he came again almost immediately. Such was the power his husband had to bring him pleasure. With a cry that probably could be heard all over Shadow Valley, Calan reared up. He was met with a louder, deeper groan, Ian's warm breath bathing his face. Warmth splashed deep inside his ass, and a whimsical thought flashed through his mind. *If I could get pregnant, that would do it.* Ian's seed was planted in fallow ground, but Calan knew that it was there. And in that moment, he also accepted that he was in love with his husband.

* * * *

Calan sipped at the cup of wine his husband held to his lips. They were sprawled against the mound of pillows, satiated from their lovemaking...for the moment. Ian was already half-aroused, and despite — or perhaps because of — the delicious ache inside his ass, Calan knew he'd be eager to be mounted again soon. The way his husband roamed his hands up and down Calan's chest, it was a guarantee. Such simple caresses were both soothing and arousing. He shook his head when Ian offered him more to drink. It would be too easy to slip off to sleep from the wine, and he wanted to savor as much of the night as he could.

Ian set the cup on the nightstand and wrapped his arms more firmly around Calan. "Are you hungry? There's some bread, cheese and honey that someone was thoughtful enough to set out for us along with the wine."

Calan couldn't help giggling. "That someone was me. As the bride, it was my responsibility to make sure we were well-provisioned for this night. You shouldn't be surprised, either. That wine and the cheese and honey are what you gave my aunt, and I made the bread from the flour and salt that you also brought."

"Huh! Your customs are finally beginning to make sense to my blockhead. Everything has a practical application as well as providing the continuity of customs. But who decked out our room with all this pretty finery?" Ian plucked up a flower petal and rubbed it against one of Calan's nipples. "Silky soft, like your skin."

Calan couldn't hold back a moan and a shudder. "That must have been the doing of the women on the council. For sure, Aunt Celia didn't bother to do it." He bit his lip as his cock started to rise. "It's usually done by the bride's friends, but I didn't expect it because I don't really have any of my own…friends that is. Not close ones, anyway. I've always been better with plants and animals than people. And it's a womanly thing to do. I may be your bride, but I'm still a boy."

Ian left the petal where it was and moved his hand down to clasp Calan's shaft. "Indeed you are. Is your ass too sore for another mounting? I can always suck this, maybe with some of that honey drizzled on it," he mused.

"Oh." Calan arched into the touch. "Do I have to choose? Can't I have both?"

Ian pinched the skin underneath Calan's cockhead, making him yelp. "Greedy boy. Whatever shall I do with you first?"

Calan had an idea of what he wanted, and Ian's playful manner made him bold. "How about…" With a quick twist that caught his husband off guard, Calan flipped himself onto his hands and knees. He turned his head to peer at his husband. "Mount me this way. I've heard it makes a cock go deeper."

That fierce look came over Ian's face once more. "I must thank your source of so much knowledge, although I must also insist that from this point forward, only I will be your teacher." He grabbed the cream and slathered his now-rock-hard-again dick before positioning himself between Calan's legs. This time, there was no gentle prep. His husband pressed the head of his cock at Calan's entrance and pushed his way in balls-deep with one long thrust.

Calan threw his head back before collapsing onto the bed. The pleasure was so unexpectedly intense, he lacked the strength to keep himself in position. It didn't matter. Ian gripped his hips with a sufficient force to keep him right where he wanted him. The man began to fuck him hard and fast, ramming his dick so deep inside Calan's ass that it was difficult to breathe. He didn't mind. Air was overrated compared to the wave of orgasm rippling up from his balls. Cum hit his heaving chest as he panted through the spasms. All the while, his husband bucked against his ass, the sound of skin slapping against skin and harsh breaths filling the room. The man was a beast galloping toward his climax. With a yell, Ian slammed against Calan's ass and ground his pelvis against it.

Calan thought he must have passed out from exhaustion for a while, because the next thing he knew, he was in Ian's arms again, his back plastered against his husband's chest.

"Are you all right, darling? I'm sorry. I fear I was too rough."

Calan shook his head. "No. It was amazing." He tilted his head in an effort to look his husband in the eye. "I'm yours now. Nothing can keep us apart."

Ian's grip tightened and he kissed the top of Calan's head. "Yes, you are…my wife. Hmm, I never thought I'd say those words."

"I like being that—your wife and not just your lover." He frowned at a thought that hadn't occurred to him before. "How shall I be known? I mean, what will people call me?"

"My dear, you are Calan, Countess of Charteris, and people will refer to you as 'my lady'. Will that bother you?"

"Not at all. It's just another way that marks me as yours." He frowned again as more questions that had formed in his mind before the marriage bubbled up to the surface. "I want to be known as myself, too, though. My reputation as an apothecary has begun to grow in Shadow Valley. I need to continue with my work, even as your wife. I'll be terrible at keeping house for you."

Ian actually laughed. "I think you'll be better than you expect, because you are a very clever boy. However, you needn't worry about such things. My household runs very well under the guidance of my housekeeper and major domo. They are the head servants," he added, wisely understanding that Calan knew nothing of all of this. "One of the reasons I offered to marry you was due to our obvious compatibility. We both like being outside, getting our hands dirty, and being worthwhile. I hate lying around Charteris Manor being waited on, and I expect you'll feel the same. Besides, the treaty gives you ultimate control over the production and delivery of the cordial. That is a heavy responsibility."

Calan felt alarmed. "Really? No one told me that."

"You mean your aunt didn't." Ian's chest rose and fell on a sigh. "One of the best things about marrying you is that I'm glad to free you of her control."

Guilt overtook his concern about his duties. "I'm afraid that's something that pleases me, too. She...she hasn't always been nice to me."

Ian tightened his hold. "I suspected as much. She's been remiss, too, I'll wager, in assuring you of your worth. I know you'll do right by the treaty and do so much more. There is much to find in Moorcondia. Who knows what medicine you might discover?"

Relieved and comforted, Calan settled more into his husband's embrace. A large yawn popped out before he could stop it. "I fear I must leave you wanting now, husband."

Ian kissed the top of his head. "Sleep, darling. I'm not such a ravenous, rutting beast that I can't wait until morning to have you again."

"Hmm. Morning sex. I hadn't realized that was a thing."

"Oh, it is, as well as afternoon sex and early evening sex. We'll try them all to see what you like best."

"I'm sure it will be impossible to choose." But as much as the idea of lying in bed all day with his husband appealed to him, there was something more that had to be done to make this marriage and the treaty successful. Knowing the power he'd been handed under the terms of the treaty, he would share his secret with the man he loved on the morrow. It was something he'd been considering since the betrothal, and now he was certain it was the right thing to do— and he didn't need the council or his aunt to tell him so.

* * * *

Calan tugged his husband up the hillside toward their destination with mounting excitement. Ian was uncharacteristically docile, allowing Calan to take charge, not telling him where they were going or why and appeared bemused by Calan's assertiveness. He seemed inclined to give him whatever he wanted so far in their marriage. Their morning had started with a vigorous bout of lovemaking, as well. There was a deep ache inside Calan's ass that he reveled in. It marked him as something new. One moment he was still a virgin and the next one, he was… not. He'd peered closely into the mirror in their room before leaving, trying to see if he looked different. While dreaming about the losing of his innocence, he'd assumed he would, that people would somehow *know*. All that had stared back at him was his usual face, albeit with brightness in his eyes that spoke of the pure joy he felt.

Once he showed Ian his secret, their bond would be complete. That was how he saw it, anyway, and for no other reason than he wanted his marriage to be based on trust as well as affection. *Love, perhaps.* It was too early to hope for that, but he did, nevertheless. It was in his nature to be exuberant, something he thought Ian liked in him. It was okay to think of such happiness without having to voice it and pressuring his husband into saying something he didn't feel. He squeezed Ian's hand with excitement as they approached the cave entrance and put away his other thoughts.

"Ah," Ian said as they entered the gloom. "I thought this would be a fun place to explore. I have a feeling, however, that you have brought me here for another reason."

Calan glanced at his husband. "Yes, I have. I need to show you something—want to do so. Over here." He continued deeper into the cave until he reached the place where water glistened down the walls and green mold covered the rocks. Without letting go of Ian's hand, he squatted and scraped a bit of the slime with his other fingers.

He held it out for Ian's inspection. "This is the basis of the medicine you seek."

Ian stayed silent for a second before cupping Calan's chin. "I haven't been privy to the entirety of the treaty, only the parts directly related to our marriage. And I know it says you will control how Moorcondia accesses the cordial, but I'm not clear that we are meant to know how to make it. This may be something for your aunt to show Isabeau, darling."

"I don't care about the politics or what my official duties are. This is my way of showing you how I trust you. This was always my discovery, not my aunts. What's mine is yours now that we're married, is it not?"

"Not really." Straightening, Ian pulled Calan back up with him. "Let us have a talk outside in the sunshine while we snack on those meat pies and cider you packed for us."

Calan grinned. "All right."

They left the cave and it was Ian's turn to lead, as was his nature. Instead of sitting on the nearest rock, he took them to the spot near the lake where they'd shared pleasure for the first time. The mere sight of it made Calan hard. He hoped the same was true for his husband. And when the man removed the satchel he carried on his shoulder and pulled Calan onto his lap, he found that it was true. Ian's cock pressed against Calan's thigh. But when he tried to turn around to straddle his lap, Ian held him in place.

"Ah, ah, my dear. I want to hear your story before we build up our appetites. What do you mean about that mold and your role in creating the cordial?"

Calan tried not to pout. It had been his idea, after all, to come out here instead of simply explaining everything back in their room. He did owe it to Ian to give him the history behind his discovery.

"You know how I like to explore and bring things back to the workshop?" When Ian nodded, he continued. "Well, we've been using various forms of moss and mold to treat wounds for some time now. It's based on generations of apothecaries trying different things. I'm always looking for something new, and last summer, I went into that cave for the first time. I found the mold, which I'd never seen before, and I brought some back to see what might be done with it."

"How do you know it has any use whatsoever? It looks to me like something that would make one sick."

Calan shrugged. "That's true of a lot of medicinals. Someone has to be willing to experiment and I have a...knack for seeing the possible use of various items I find occurring naturally."

Ian frowned. "You've said that before and I believe it, but you didn't try this stuff on yourself, did you?"

With a chuckle, Calan shook his head. "No, of course not. First I fashioned it into a paste, then I happened upon a patient of sorts to try it on because there was nothing left to lose. Remember the neighbor's dog, Benny? The poor thing cut its paw on something, and despite efforts with known creams, it became infected. Trying this new paste was a last-ditch effort. And it worked!" Calan couldn't hold back his excitement, reliving the day when he'd found that the dog was getting better. "After that, I started efforts to distill the essence of it to determine whether it had healing properties when taken by mouth. If the infection can be fought from the inside before it even manifests, then that's the best outcome. The result was the cordial you've heard so much about."

"Such a clever wife I have." Ian's sincerity showed through his eyes.

Calan lowered his gaze in sudden shyness. He wasn't used to being complimented, not really. By the time his new cordial had been introduced to the council, Aunt Celia had taken credit for the discovery. She always said he only knew as much as she'd taught him. No doubt the others on the council thought he didn't know enough to recreate it using Moorcondian ingredients. "It wasn't anything any good apothecary wouldn't have figured out."

"Hmm," was all Ian said. Then, first brushing a few flyaway strands of hair from Calan's face, he asked, "Do you think this mold is unique to Shadow Valley or even just to this cave?"

Calan shook his head. "No, I don't. The conditions for its growth should be found in many places." He bit his lip. "I don't know what the treaty says, but I don't expect that Moorcondia will be dependent on Shadow Valley producing the cordial and shipping it. We don't have enough qualified people to mass-produce it. I had assumed the agreement involves giving your people the formula for it. Do you think I'm wrong about that?" His decision to show Ian the source of the medicine had been premised on the idea of the treaty giving Moorcondia the ability to make its own stores. And if he were expected to somehow oversee its production without giving the formula away...well, it simply wasn't possible.

"I honestly have no idea. That is all Isabeau's domain. But I can assure you, darling, that I won't use your trust in me to undermine the provisions in the treaty that benefit Shadow Valley."

Perhaps his husband's reassurance shouldn't be so comforting. It was, though. Calan had no doubt about the man's sense of honor. "I'm here because I do...trust you, that is." A thought occurred to him. "Will we do any traveling or will my explorations for new medicines be limited to your lands?"

"You will find my lands vast and varied. There is much of it beyond the part that is cultivated that I, myself, have never ventured. We'll do so together." He pressed a soft kiss against Calan's cheek. "And I'll endeavor to take you to as many places as I can. So long as you're with me, I expect to be content no matter what we do or where we go."

His husband's words warmed him and encouraged his arousal. He wanted to feel Ian's cock driven deep inside him. There was something else, however, that enticed him almost as much. Calan slid out of Ian's loose embrace and, forcing his legs apart, knelt before him. The discomfort of the rocky ground was easily ignored in favor of his goal. When he reached for Ian's belt, he stopped him by clasping his hands.

"Whatever are you up to, darling?"

Calan let his passion show through his expression. "I want to taste you. Is that all right?"

Ian's answer was merely a grunt. He let go of Calan and pressed his palms against the rock. At the same time, he splayed his legs even more, giving Calan easier access to where he wanted to go. This time, when he reached to unbuckle Ian's belt, there was no resistance. The man had to help him put it aside, along with the scabbard and heavy sword. The laces to his trousers were easy to undo, though, and once they were, Ian's dick sprang free. The large cockhead glistened with pre-cum. The shaft was warm and twitched when Calan clasped it with one hand. It was so thick he couldn't quite encircle it fully with his fingers and thumb. The dick would be hard to take, but Calan relished the effort it would take to try.

He moistened his lips as he shuffled as close as he could get. Then he leaned over and licked Ian's slit. That effort elicited an encouraging grunt. The salty tang of cum wet Calan's appetite for more. He opened his mouth wide and enveloped the head. That small amount of the cock was almost the limit of what he could take in. But he was determined to please his husband in this way, knowing from his own experience that it was amazing. So he pressed down, flattening his tongue and relaxing his throat, while using his hand to jerk the shaft. Still, he gagged almost immediately and was forced to retreat for a few seconds. Undaunted, he breathed deeply through his nose and tried again, forcing the dick even farther.

Ian carded his fingers through Calan's hair and pulled his head up. "Darling, please. I find no pleasure in hurting you or making you sick."

Calan peered up at him. "This is the best treat I've ever had. Please let me gorge myself however I wish. I promise this is no hardship."

Ian's cock pulsed and danced within his grip. Without saying a word, he used his fingers to lower Calan's head once more, allowing him to suck the dick back into his mouth.

This time, Calan tried for quality over quantity. He had a whole lifetime to train himself to swallow all of Ian's dick—and he *would* someday. That was the silent vow he made as he worked the cockhead and a bit of the shaft with his tongue, laving the skin and even using his teeth to scrape lightly. The effect was obvious. The cock seemed to swell within his mouth before cum spurted out. It flooded Calan's mouth, making him choke once more. But when Ian tried to pull away, Calan stayed with him, swallowing as fast as he could. Still, some cum dribbled out, and when he finally released the dick entirely, he sat back on his heels and licked his lips clean.

"Gods, what you do to me!" Ian stared at him with half-closed eyes, his nostrils flared and his chest heaving with deep breaths. Grabbing Calan by the shoulders, he hauled him back to his lap and kissed him deeply.

Calan curled around his husband, plastering himself against the man's large, hard body and trying to suck in his tongue as he had the cock. He gasped when Ian gripped him by the crotch. He was bucking into the hold, coming with overwhelming force before his mind even registered the touch. When it was done, he lay breathless within Ian's embrace, his head pressed against the man's throat.

His husband nuzzled the top of his head. "I've never known anyone as sensitive to sex as you, darling. You come from my fucking you alone, have you noticed? I barely have to touch you to make you climax, too. I feel rather cheated in how little I get to play with your body. Maybe I should put you in chastity to teach you self-control. What do you think of that idea?" There was amusement in his tone.

Calan had no idea what the man was talking about and yet his cock jerked at the suggestion. He snuggled closer. "Whatever you want, Ian. I'm yours to do with as you wish."

Chapter Eight

Ian returned to the village with his wife's hand in his and visions of putting the boy's lovely cock and balls under lock and key. Calan was not only amazingly responsive to his touch, but also open to whatever Ian wanted to do, a rare thing in a lover in his experience. It had taken a great deal of his own self-control not to fuck the boy as he sat on his lap. And that was after the stupefying blow job. He couldn't get enough of his wife and that was fine by him. He hoped that would never change, even as they grew old together. Well, not exactly together. Ian had a good head start on Calan. It made him realize that he needed to consult with his solicitor to make sure that Calan was well-cared for once Ian was gone.

As the dowager countess, the boy would always be entitled to the means to live out the rest of his life in comfort, but Calan wasn't going to be content with puttering around the Charteris estate. He would want freedom, and Ian was determined that he would always have what he wanted. After all, however much Calan enjoyed the physical side of marriage, it was still true that Ian had forced the issue by offering it as part of the treaty. It was his duty to make sure Calan was happy and occupied with things he enjoyed. To that end, he had already decided that his wife would have a workshop and be encouraged to spend his days much as he already did. Who knew? The boy might discover something even more miraculous growing in Moorcondia.

That thought, along with the longhouse coming into view, reminded him how Calan had trusted him with the very secret the mission had been based on, not that Ian had any idea what one did with the mold he'd been shown to turn it into medicine. Knowing where to start was at least half the battle, and it was humbling that his wife believed the knowledge was safe with him. He would not abuse that trust, no matter what. Besides, Isabeau was responsible for making the best deal for Moorcondia. He had to believe she'd done her job well.

His sister came out of the longhouse at that moment, the Shadow Valley council by her side and in her wake. The atmosphere was convivial, although Isabeau hadn't lost her stern demeanor, and Celia's expression was only a lighter shade of grim. He hoped the treaty had been signed, sealed and delivered, bound by the matrimonial tie between him and his wife. Not that he had any more idea of its exact terms than Calan. He supposed now was as good a time as any to actually find out beyond the bare bones he'd bothered with to date. It was possible that everything from this point forward involved matters left to others and all he needed to focus on was making his marriage a happy one. Something told him that was wishful thinking.

Plastering a smile on his face, he led Calan over to the group. "Good afternoon. May I offer my congratulations on your concluded negotiations?"

Fennic was the first to respond, the man truly having a happy and kind personality. "Yes, thank you, my lord. Lady Isabeau has been most generous in what your great country has to offer our humble one." The man's gaze slid over to Calan. "And we, of course, are honored by the new familial connection with such a powerful family." He paused, and his cheeks pinked a bit. "I trust the happy couple has enjoyed…the morning?" He may as well have asked if Ian and Calan had fucked.

Ian squeezed his wife's hand before answering for the both of them. "Quite so. Our bridal chamber was charmingly welcoming, the perfect place for us to begin our marriage. And Calan has been showing me to a few of his favorite spots before he is to leave them for his new home."

Before anyone could offer up any further niceties, Celia pushed forward. "What is this?" She turned a furious face at Calan. "Have you given him our secrets?"

Ian tugged Calan closer to his side, letting go of his hand in order to embrace him by the waist. "I can assure you, madam, that Calan has done no more or less than a loyal wife should." Apparently, the issue of the treaty terms had been forced to the here and now. Ian wanted to shield Calan from any unpleasantness, but he had as much right as anyone—if not more—to hear what had been agreed to. "And as Calan's husband, I need to know what the terms of the treaty are that affect him beyond our marriage as the person who developed the cordial." He glared at Celia, daring her to contradict him.

Isabeau stiffened. "I'm not sure this is the time or place for those details, brother."

"I beg to differ, sister. My marriage is less than a day old and as the instigator of this outcome, I'm not simply a casual observer. Not anymore."

Fennic jumped in, almost literally, the brave man standing between two formidable women. "We intend to announce the treaty terms this evening at your farewell banquet, my lord, but I see no reason why we shouldn't do so for your and your wife's benefit now. After all," he added with a kindly glance at Calan, "your wife *is* central to the terms."

Ian merely lifted an eyebrow at the man.

Fennic cleared his throat. "So, um, one of the main problems we faced was that Shadow Valley is a self-sustaining country with no significant exporting of our goods. While we recognize the importance of having sufficient quantity of the cordial to benefit the larger population of Moorcondia, we simply cannot manage to produce that ourselves."

"Which is why Moorcondia wanted the formula from the beginning," Isabeau said.

Fennic nodded. "Just so. And while we believe your king to be true to his word, we were…concerned that if we simply give away the formula, the incentive to provide the trade goods in return would become…less urgent."

If Ian had ever doubted the savviness of the Shadow Valley council, this confession eliminated it. The king was a man of his word, but why should these people believe that? Without the ongoing benefit being offered by one side of a trade deal, there was always the possibility that the other side would lose interest in keeping the bargain. "I can see where that would be a sticking point," Ian offered in a conciliatory tone.

"But with your marriage to Calan? Well, that did cut through the problem nicely, my lord." He beamed at the boy. "You won't only be in charge of the distribution of the cordial. The formula will travel to your new home inside your head and you may share it with whomever you deem necessary for its proper production. We assume you'll have no trouble replicating it, but if you need your aunt's help before you leave...?"

"I don't." Calan's tone was unusually biting for him.

Fennic didn't seem to notice or was too good a politician to show that he had. "Excellent, and Charteris will become the hub of its manufacturing, benefiting from the revenue it will generate. We trust that the count now has a personal interest in making sure that the treaty terms are met, and all will be well." The man clasped his hands in obvious delight and swung his gaze around to everyone gathered.

Isabeau looked less pleased as she confirmed the outcome. "Yes, that is what the treaty says. Your wife is to have control over the production of the cordial and is entitled to half of all of its profits. If the raw materials cannot be found in Moorcondia, you must send some of your people here to harvest it, however often as is necessary."

Ian gave into the urge to kiss the top of his wife's head before commenting. "Of course, Calan will have the freedom to do whatever he likes as an apothecary and I've already agreed that his money is his own. That was never in doubt, and he and I discussed it during our walk."

Celia took a half-step closer to Calan. "But you've already told him everything he needs to know, haven't you boy? They don't require your cooperation. You've damned the treaty for the sake of your carnal pleasure. Now he has your body and our valuable cordial."

Calan jerked within his embrace. Ian moved him away from his aunt, tightening his hold in an effort to reassure him. "I must insist, madam, that you direct your ire at me. Calan has done nothing to earn it, and I don't take kindly to anyone impugning the actions and motives of my family — especially when it comes to my wife." He took a second and a deep breath to calm himself. "No harm has been done to the treaty or the interests of either country." He wasn't in the habit of intimidating women, but he stared at Celia until she looked away.

Ever the peacemaker, Fennic interjected. "Of course, my lord. No one intended to imply otherwise. We understand that there should be no secrets between husband and wife. And to that point, my own wife and I would like to extend an invitation for you to lunch at our home, a more personal event than eating in the longhouse. Lady Isabeau and her adorable daughter included, of course."

Ian would have just as soon spent the meal alone with Calan, but the boy had other ideas.

"That's a very generous offer, Councillor Fennic. My husband I would be delighted to join you. Wouldn't we, Ian?" He looked at him with a kind of pleading in his eyes. The whole interaction with his aunt had obviously upset him.

"Whatever you wish, darling."

"Yes," Isabeau added. "Most kind of you."

"Excellent." Fennic's beaming smile only dimmed somewhat when he glanced at Celia.

The woman scowled. "I have work to do. After all, my apprentice is now lost to me. I shall have to labor extra hard to care for our people." With that, she turned on her heel and strode away.

"Please excuse her," Calan said in a low voice. "This is very hard for her, I'm sure."

"We shall miss you, my boy, but Moorcondia is going to be a generous trading partner. Shall we meet at the top of the next hour?"

Isabeau confirmed with a shallow curtesy and waited until the man left before speaking again. "Honestly, Ian, it's a good thing you never went in for diplomacy. Could you not have kept your morning's activities to yourself?"

Ian shrugged. "She's the one that jumped to conclusions, and I am never going to hide what I do with my wife in the shadows."

Calan pressed his face into Ian's shoulder. "I'm sorry I caused trouble."

"You did nothing of the kind, darling." He shot his sister a warning look. "Celia doesn't like losing Calan because she has robbed him of his ideas and has tried to take credit where she shouldn't. I don't think anyone has been fooled as much as she thinks, on that score. And neither Calan nor I shall do anything contrary to the treaty."

"I trust you, naturally, on that point, brother." She didn't include Calan in that reassurance, but Ian let it slide. "I'll get you a copy of the treaty after we lunch with Fennic, so that you and your…wife will know all that has been agreed to."

"Thank you. Now, we must wash the dirt of the forest off us before eating. We'll meet you outside your room and walk to Fennic's together, shall we?"

Isabeau pursed her lips. "Yes. We are family, after all." With a dubious look toward Calan, she left.

"I don't like people being mad at each other."

Ian hauled Calan up by his shoulders to kiss him soundly before easing him back down again. "Some people are always going to find a reason to be angry or upset. Don't let it bother you, Calan. You and I are happy together, are we not?"

"Oh yes." The boy's eyes went wide, and a shiver ran through him. "If the last few days have been any indication, I expect to always want to be by your side."

Ian chuckled. "When you look at me that way, wife, it gives me bad ideas."

"On the contrary, husband, I believe they are good ones." His pupils dilated as he spoke, and Ian didn't need to feel the boy's dick to know it was hard.

The gods knew Ian was fully aroused again. "I think, if we are very quick, we can do something about those ideas as we wash up. What do you think?"

"That we are wasting time." With that, Calan grabbed his hand and led him away.

* * * *

Ian and his bride stumbled into their chamber, not drunk from the interminable banquet that Fennic had hosted to send them off in the morning with great revelry, but clumsy with their greedy efforts to disrobe each other. He took the lead by sweeping the boy up into his arms and tossing him onto the bed. He only bothered to rid himself of his belt and sword before tumbling down with him, covering the lithe body with his own, pawing at everything that he could reach, while robbing them both of breath with a never-ending kiss. His dick was a shaft of rock, poking at the thin cloth of his trousers with enough force that he expected it to rip through any moment. Reaching between their writhing bodies, he freed the demanding thing and immediately humped against Calan's leg.

The boy whimpered in what Ian already recognized as a plea to take him—fast. Ian had meant it when he'd said his wife was more sexual than any lover he'd ever had. The boy was fearless in his eagerness and unabashed in what he wanted. And he made sure he was prepared. Ian had watched with mounting desire while Calan had lined his own ass with cream before dressing for dinner. The little flirt had fluttered his lashes and said he was too eager for Ian's cock to have to wait for it.

Ian had wanted to bend him over the nearest bench as they'd left the longhouse. It had been torture to wait until they were behind closed doors. Now that they were, he wasn't going to hold back in some misplaced sense of chivalry or civilized control. His need for his wife was primal, urgent and unstoppable, and the thinking part of him said that Calan deserved the respect to believe he knew what was best for himself. He broke off the kiss and twisted Calan over so that he lay on his belly. Then he pushed the boy's trousers down only enough to expose his adorable ass and plunged into it. Calan cried out and threw back his head at the sudden and hard breach. Ian sunk his teeth into the bottom of the boy's neck to hold him in place. A few thrusts was all it took to send him over the edge. He growled and shook his mouth as he emptied himself.

Calan quivered beneath him, squeezing his hole to milk the last of the cum out of Ian's dick. There was nothing truly passive about this boy, even when he was nailed by a cock embedded inside him, while a large body imprisoned him to the spot. He was more than a mere vessel for Ian's passion. He demanded and took as much as he received. Despite his position and power, Ian felt ensnared by the boy, and he was happier to be in that place than he'd ever been before. *This is who I've always been waiting for.*

As marvelous as it was to lie on top of his wife with his cock cocooned by wet heat, he knew he risked crushing Calan, and the boy had to be sore for being mounted so often. He reluctantly pulled out and rolled over. Then when he regained sufficient strength, he undressed them both properly and positioned his wife against the pillows.

Calan looked at him with heavy-lidden eyes. "That was worth waiting for. All during those boring speeches, I kept imagining your cock inside me. I want it there still."

Ian practically choked on his spit. "You are a menace, darling. Allow this old man to regain his strength." When Calan snorted at that remark, Ian grinned. "I'm thirsty. How about you?" He sauntered over to the small table that was once again filled with small bites of food and a decanter of a dark liquid. He picked it up. "What's this?"

"Brandywine. Mistress Emelda makes it in small batches. How kind of her to provide us with some."

"Ah. I happen to like the version made in Moorcondia." Unstopping the decanter, he sniffed the liquid before pouring a glass. "Do you want some?"

"No, thanks. It's too strong for my tastes. I'm not thirsty anyway…unless you count my craving for your cum."

In the midst of sipping the brandywine, Ian spit some of it out. He whipped his head around. "You little beast! Remind me not to eat or drink anything without gagging you first." He put the glass down, the warmth of the drink seeping into his belly. He took only a moment to wipe his dick clean from the remnants of the fucking. He wanted Calan to always enjoy the taste of him.

Keeping his gaze on his wife, he all but leaped onto the bed to straddle the boy. He trapped Calan's arms to his side, using his legs to hold him in place. "Open up, greedy boy." Calan stared at him without flinching as he opened his mouth wide.

It took effort for Ian to stay in control as he fed his dick into that welcoming warmth. He didn't stop until he bumped the opening to Calan's throat, making the boy gag. Although the urge to keep going was strong, rational thought prevailed. He pulled back to give Calan a chance to breathe, then thrust his dick to the back of Calan's mouth again. It went a little deeper this time, and he'd have to be content with that. His wife's lips were spread wide around his shaft, stretched obscenely. Calan's eyes watered and yet he tried to keep them open. That proved impossible once Ian started face-fucking him in earnest. In and out, he drilled with his dick, grabbing the headboard for leverage. Calan was present as always, not simply taking it, but laving Ian's cock with his tongue and sucking, even as Ian forced the shaft farther down his throat.

With a roar, Ian came again, flooding that small mouth with so much cum, one would have thought he hadn't orgasmed in months. He forced his eyes back open to watch how his cum dribbled past Calan's lips. As he pulled his dick out, he sat flush against Calan's groin and rocked. The boy's cock swelled against his ass and released itself. Once again, they lay entangled in each other's arms, spent.

* * * *

Calan quietly put a topped-up glass of brandywine and a slice of the bread he'd baked, slathered with butter and honey on the table by the bed. He liked the idea of leaving his husband a small meal that he'd had a hand in making. It was a more intimate form of caretaking than he was used to as a healer and a small way of supporting a powerful man. Ian had everything at his fingertips. There would be little for Calan to do once they returned to Charteris that wasn't already being done by someone else. Right here and now, he had the opportunity to pamper his man in private.

As Calan turned away from the bed, Ian shot his hand out and grabbed him by the arm. "Where are you going, darling?"

Calan smiled at the sleepy question. "I want to go back to my workshop and gather some more things to take with me. I was a bit rushed before and perhaps muddle-headed from our…you know, time in the forest." He blushed at the thought of all the ways he and Ian had made love. He wondered whether he would ever become sanguine to such matters.

Ian squeezed once before letting go. "Hurry back, wife."

A warmth of arousal spread through his groin. "Yes, husband. There's food and drink here if you want." He slipped out of the room and headed outside.

He half-expected one of the constant guards to stop him from leaving. Instead, one of them stepped to his side and walked with him.

Calan stopped. "Oh, that's not necessary. I mean I'm fine on my own."

"Your pardon, Countess, but the count has given very explicit orders. You are to have at least one guard accompany you at all times — for your safety, of course," the man added with a shallow bow.

"I see." He supposed he would have to get used to the idea that he was no longer simply a boy helping his aunt. He was of the Moorcondian nobility, and they apparently were used to being surrounded by protectors and servants wherever they went. "Thank you."

In the early dawn of the day, there weren't many people around. That served Calan's mood. He wanted a quiet moment to say his good-byes to his homeland, and it proved easy to ignore the presence of the soldier in his wake. If he thought too much of how he was about to leave the only place he'd ever known, he might cry. That wouldn't do. He was happy — deliriously so — and didn't want anyone to misinterpret his mood. Far from being a sacrifice to his people's needs, he felt blessed to be married to a man who treated him with such care and brought him to a level of pleasure that he couldn't have dreamed of. It was hard to leave Shadow Valley, but exciting, too. He had no doubt his new life would be filled with adventure simply because it *was* new.

As he slipped into the workshop, he made a mental list of what he wanted. Ian had said there was plenty of room for Calan to take whatever he desired. Still, Calan had prioritized his personal belongings and now having seen the size of the storage carriage, felt confident that there was room for a couple more baskets worth of dried flora and pastes. He would only be taking his own stock, nothing of his aunts, so he pushed away any guilt over what he intended.

He pulled up short when he saw that Celia was already in there. "I-I'm sorry, Aunt. I hadn't realized you'd be here." She was an early riser, yet typically went foraging first thing if she wasn't visiting the sick.

Celia looked over her shoulder and continued to pound something in her mortar. "What are *you* doing here? I would have thought the count holds you on a short leash to keep you handy to slake his lust, not that I expect you to want to stray too far from his bed." Her words were spoken matter-of-factly and yet there was an obvious undertone of disapproval if not disgust.

"I'm not a prisoner, Aunt." He strove for patience, understanding that his leaving was hard on her.

"Really? Tell that to the man looming behind you. I'll wager the count won't let you go anywhere by yourself now."

"That's probably true, but only because he's worried about my safety. This marriage will be a successful one on a personal level, I believe, as well as benefiting our people. I'm happy," he added, not sure if that made a difference to the woman. *Probably not.*

Aunt Celia turned with her fists planted on her hips. The look she gave him was terrible. "No doubt, being in the man's bed pleases you very much. As for what's best for our country? Don't take me for a fool. Once

Moorcondia has you under your husband's thumb in their territory, you will have to give them everything they want. They'll pry the formula out of your head no matter what you decide, and you'll be good for nothing more than to warm the count's bed. The treaty will be useless. And anything new you create will belong to them and them alone. Shadow Valley will never benefit from your healing gifts again."

Calan frowned. "No, that's not true! The Moorcondians are honorable people. Ian married me to make the treaty stronger, not to subvert it. And I would never betray my country like that. While it's true that I will always explore and experiment to find new medicinals, Ian says the treaty requires Moorcondia to share them with others. You must know that, given how you were there when it was drafted. I'll make sure the terms are complied with."

"If you believe that you have any choice or control over your life, now, you are naïve to a dangerous degree. I won't be there to help you when you find out that your husband owns you and can do as he likes, regardless of what you want."

She turned her back to him again and leaned on the table, muttering under her breath. "There is no hope for it. It had to be done. You must be protected for your own sake as well as for the rest of us. In time, you will see that this is all for your protection as much as anyone else's. You belong in Shadow Valley."

Unease shot through him. He took a step closer to Celia. "What are you saying? What do you mean? Ian and I are leaving this morning. I'm going to Moorcondia."

"Did you really think his sister was going to let that happen or that I would stand idly by while you were turned against me?" She shot him a look over her shoulder that froze his blood. Her expression was one of vile satisfaction. "She has acted rashly, but I had no reason to stop her, quite the opposite. Eventually, you will understand that what has been done was for the best."

Calan wasted no more time with questions or even thinking. He ran out of the workshop and raced back to Ian's room. The stout soldier stayed hot on his heels, not questioning the rush.

"Get Lady Isabeau," he shouted to one of the Moorcondian guards standing by the doors. It was instinct that had him demanding her. She was Ian's sister and therefore someone he trusted to help his husband, no matter what his aunt had implied.

He gasped as he entered the room. Ian hung halfway off the bed, his shoulders heaving with labored breadth, one arm dangling over the floor where the goblet of brandywine had shattered.

"Ian!" Calan gave no thought to the broken glass as he flung himself to his husband's side. He grunted as he tried to lift the man back fully onto the bed. "Help me," he shouted to the soldier who was still following him.

The large man had no trouble replacing Ian onto the bed and was sensitive enough to immediately back away to give Calan room to sit beside his husband. Ian's skin was pasty and shiny with sweat. His body trembled, and his lips were parted in a kind of rictus. His struggle to breathe was even more obvious. Calan's mind scattered with terror. His husband was dying, poisoned. There was no doubt in his mind what was happening, yet he couldn't manage to think what to do, despite his training as an apothecary. Ian was going to die right before his eyes. *How will I live without him?* It was only when Isabeau burst into the room that he was able to marshal his thoughts.

"What is this?" The Moorcondian woman clasped the top of her robe tightly to her neck as she joined Calan at the bedside. Her hair was in a loose braid, and he doubted any man had ever seen her in such casual attire since her husband's death. She didn't seem to care, having clearly just risen from her bed. She didn't wait for an answer, either, dropping to her knees and picking up what was left of the cup. She sniffed its contents. "What was in this?" Her expression was fierce as she glared at him.

Calan shook his head. "I don't know. I smelled nothing when I poured it."

"And you didn't drink any?" Her tone was suspicious, and he didn't blame her.

"No. The decanter was here when we returned from supper. I didn't think anything of it. Leaving gifts of food and drink for the newly wedded couple is the custom. And I didn't drink any of it because I don't like brandywine. Most people would have no reason to know that, though." That was then he was sure of what had happened, not that his aunt's words had really given him any doubt. He looked at Lady Isabeau. "Do you have an emetic? I think purging is the best thing to do, regardless of what poison was used, and I dare not take the time to return to my workshop for some."

Ian's sister hesitated only a second. "Fetch my medicine bag." She shot the order to the maid who had come with her before using her hem to sweep away the shards of glass. She pulled the chamber pot out from under the bed. "We run the risk of damaging his throat and mouth by bringing it back up, but without knowing what it is, you're right that we have no choice. Ah, here," she said when the maid returned.

Calan held his husband's hand, wiping sweaty hair from his brow and feeling useless as his sister-by-marriage processed the emetic. But when Isabeau returned with a cup of liquid, she handed it to him to administer, instead of doing so herself. The show of trust and the recognition of Calan's rights as a wife chased away any doubt he had about the woman's intentions. But Ian hadn't gotten any lighter, so he needed her help to raise him to a sitting position. Then he poured the contents down Ian's throat. The huge man was hard to maneuver, limp as he was. They managed together to get him leaning over the side of the bed once he started to react to the medicine and his stomach emptied into the pot. The sounds were horrible. Calan felt as if he were killing the man, not saving him. He forced such thoughts out of his head and made himself think as a healer and not someone watching his beloved fight for his life.

Don't die! I promise to tell you how I feel if you just live. Ian had to survive this. He *had* to.

Chapter Nine

Calan ran the cool cloth over Ian's hot skin. He was in and out of consciousness, feverish and restless. But he was still alive as midday approached. That was something. The purging of his stomach had helped, and his husband's body had expelled more of the poison on its own. It had been slow-acting, the sip or two he'd taken before they had made love having worked its way through him before the symptoms started in earnest. Calan and Lady Isabeau had quietly cleaned his man. It was during that wordless effort that Calan had come to appreciate the professionalism of the woman and to understand why the King of Moorcondia had put his faith in her. She had to be as worried as Calan was about Ian's fight for survival and maybe even embarrassed over touching her naked brother, yet she gave no outward sign of such feelings. She had left the more intimate parts to Calan, which he appreciated. He hadn't been married long, but he already felt as if the man were *his* and no one else's.

They made Ian as comfortable as possible while they waited. Waited. Waited. Calan had sat by the bedsides of sick people often when helping his aunt. It had always been hard watching others suffer and worrying that they might succumb to illness. Death had been awful, as well, and caused him to feel guilt, even though his aunt had always said that they could only do their best and accept that they weren't gods to give and take life. Now he knew, though, that whatever he'd felt had been nothing compared with what loved ones had endured. His mind recoiled any time he envisioned Ian dying.

Isabeau appeared in his peripheral vision and placed the back of her hand against Ian's forehead. "I don't think the fever is abating. We have to do more to fight the poison. I'm just not sure what. I've checked all my medicinals but only brought the basics to treat injuries and general illnesses while on the road. And I can't be certain what will help anyway, because I don't know what he ingested. The wrong thing might make his condition worse."

A sharp pain stabbed Calan's heart. "Yes. I've also been thinking on it. There is something I can try—a combination of medicinals that each help different poisons. I believe that with the right doses, together they might act as a more universal antidote, although I've had no opportunity to put the idea to the test. Thank the gods, poisonings are few and far between and always accidental, but sometimes kids don't understand what they've ingested and something generic to treat them would be a great help. I've been reluctant to do so now with Ian's life in the balance, hoping the poison had been dispelled enough to save him."

Isabeau narrowed her gaze. "You're not referring to something involving the cordial that brought us here?"

Calan shook his head. "No. That's only useful against infection. This is…something else, something I've been fiddling with for some years." He blinked back tears. "It might not work, or…" He couldn't say the words.

"It could kill him." It wasn't a question. Lady Isabeau was no fool. "Do it."

"How can I take that risk?" The thought that he might be the one to end Ian's life was intolerable.

"To do nothing and watch the poison that's left in his body overwhelm him is no better a solution. At least if we try, we'll know we did all we could."

"You trust me?" He knew the woman disapproved of the marriage, of him.

Isabeau looked away and inhaled deeply once before turning back to him. "No matter what your aunt has said in the matter, I believe that it was you who concocted the cordial that will save so many Moorcondian lives. However I might feel about your marrying my brother, I have no doubt about your apothecary skills. And," she said, closing her eyes briefly, "I can see how much you love him. Please do whatever you think will work. No matter the outcome, I will always value your effort."

Calan stared at his husband, forcing himself to see the suffering. "Thank you." He slid off the bed and put on his boots. "Will you please send a few of your guards with me? One is probably enough, but I…don't want to risk any interference." He hated thinking that his aunt might try to stop him. Worse, he feared she would have turned others against Ian and Isabeau, who could keep him from returning out of a misplaced sense of protection.

Lady Isabeau didn't ask the why of his request. She simply instructed the burly soldier who'd stuck by him before to round up more to go with him. Four men surrounded him as he hurried to his workshop. The weight of their presence bolstered Calan's confidence as he passed many of the people he knew. They stopped and stared as he went by them, yet no one tried to interfere with his journey or talk to him. Better still, Aunt Celia was nowhere to be seen when he arrived. He wasted no time going to the three jars standing in a cluster on the table where he processed his concoctions. One guard stepped inside the room with him, a silent sentry. Seeing him there and knowing that the others were outside made Calan feel safe and allowed him to concentrate on only the task at hand.

He stared at the bottles for a few seconds as he called up his idea of how to employ them. There was nothing new about any of them, their usage for various poisons having spanned the ages. It was his ideas of how to marry them with one another that was novel. If only he knew exactly what Celia had used, but she would never tell him and there were too many possibilities. He needed to introduce something to bind the poison, neutralize it, then protect the organs in Ian's body that were being attacked. He believed that a combination of what he had before him would work overall, regardless of what it fought, and while he abhorred the idea of testing his theories on his husband, Lady Isabeau had been right. Doing nothing came with at least the same amount of risk. *What would Ian do?* The answer was easy. The man was a fighter. He'd take action.

Resolved, Calan went about processing his ingredients. It was all guesswork as to how much of each to use, but he was *good* at this. He knew that. If not, he'd never have met Ian in the first place. As tempting as it was to dither and re-think everything he'd done, Calan forced himself to trust that his instincts had allowed him to do it right the first time. He slipped the ground ingredients into a pouch, clutched it in his hand—and stopped.

Aunt Celia appeared in the doorway leading to the main house. The inside guard rushed over to block her with silent resolve. She pushed at the man, but of course it was like an ant trying to move a mountain. "Let me pass, you oaf! This is my property, and you are both trespassers." She slapped at the man's chest to no avail.

The guard slowly turned his head to look at Calan over his shoulder. "Countess?"

It took Calan a few seconds to realize that the man was asking him what to do. The title he used and the deference in his tone was so casually given that it stunned Calan and made him realize for the first time that through his marriage, he had gained real status and power. The man wasn't merely following his count's or Lady Isabeau's orders. He expected Calan to issue them as well. If this man was anything to go by, the people of Moorcondia would accept him as Ian's wife, the Countess of Charteris. It wasn't some game being played to get Calan into Ian's bed and to secure access to the cordial. Calan's life had really changed, and the knowledge of it gave him courage.

He lifted his chin. "Let her pass."

The guard stepped to one side without hesitation, although he stood facing Calan with his hand on the hilt of his sword.

Celia sailed in, her gaze narrowed on the pouch Calan clutched. "What is this you're doing?"

"Trying to save my husband, as you well know." He took a step toward her. "Help me by telling me what you gave him." With her here, he had to at least try to get an answer out of her.

With a sniff, Celia stood with her hands on her hips. "Nothing. Whatever is happening to that man is not of my doing. I've told you to look to his sister. My involvement was only being silent about what I saw, and I don't regret it. Your marriage was always a mistake, and I'm glad she's rectifying it." Her lips curled into a nasty smile. "You've left her with him, I'll wager. She's probably finishing the job as we speak."

Despite Calan being sure that Isabeau was not responsible for the poisoning, his heart skipped a beat, and the urge to run back to his husband was strong. He held his ground, instead. "You're lying. I know you poisoned the brandywine. Tell me what you used! Please," he added in a near whisper, pride being nothing compared to Ian's life.

"I can't help you." Her voice was flat, her gaze cold.

Calan was tempted to tell the guard to grab his aunt to shake the truth out of her, but he wasn't a violent person, and he doubted the effort would do any good. He could see the fervor in his aunt's eyes. The woman was convinced she'd done no wrong. He was wasting time talking to her. He hurried from the room, giving Celia a wide berth to ensure she didn't try to take the pouch from him. This time, he ran full tilt through the village, the guards keeping up with him and not breaking their protective formation. When he arrived back in the room, a quick glance told him that Ian was no better—but also no worse, which was something.

What he held in his hand would tip the balance, one way or the other. He pushed aside his fear and hardened his resolve even more as he went to Isabeau, who sat beside her brother.

"I need hot water." He held up the pouch. "These should be steeped."

Isabeau jumped to her feet, her nightgown and robe fluttering around her, testament that her devotion to her brother was so great that she still hadn't taken time to make herself more presentable. "I'll see to it."

Calan placed a hand on his husband's hot chest. "Hang on, my love. Please," he added, hating the sound of fear in his voice. Ian didn't need to hear that.

When Isabeau returned with her maid hefting a steaming kettle, Calan went to join her. The maid put the kettle on the food table and stood back to give them room. Together, Calan and Isabeau mixed the medicine in the hot water and waited. It was hard. Calan wanted to use it as quickly as possible, yet he knew that if the infusion was too weak, it wouldn't help Ian as much as it was intended to. He went to bathe his husband's face once more while Isabeau paced. Finally, she tapped Calan on the shoulder and gestured for him to go over to the table.

He peered into the kettle and sniffed. "I think it's been steeping long enough." He glanced at Ian. "It's hard to say, but…"

Isabeau put her hand on his arm. "Don't second-guess yourself. You know what you are doing, but if it helps, I agree with you. It's time."

Calan poured some of the drink into a cup and swishing it around, blew into it to render it sufficiently cool so as not to burn Ian's mouth. He looked at Isabeau. "I'm going to need your help."

"Of course."

Once again, they managed to put Ian in a sitting position to force liquid down his throat. As the man sputtered and swallowed, Calan prayed he wasn't killing his husband.

* * * *

Isabeau returned to the room, having finally left to dress for the day. She was in a simple frock with her hair still braided down her back. This was how he imagined the woman looked on a daily basis when she wasn't obligated to play the king's emissary. He liked it. It made it easier to see her as she really was and understand Ian's unfailing affection for her. This was a woman who cared more about doing what was needed without worrying about her lofty place in society. With her words and actions this morning, he knew without a doubt that she also loved her brother. She could have told her guards to remove him from his husband's side, as well. He had no doubt that they would obey the woman over him. That she had instead deferred to Calan confirmed that however she felt about his marriage, she wasn't going to hold it against him.

She placed her hand on Ian's cheek. "I think his fever has abated."

Calan exhaled sharply. He'd thought so, too, but didn't trust his judgment wasn't merely wishful thinking. "He does feel cooler and seems less restless."

"Your concoction has worked, and for that, we can be thankful." She stared directly into Calan's eyes. "*I* am thankful. I honestly don't believe I could have saved him myself."

"He had only a couple of sips of the brandywine when we first arrived and doesn't seem to have drunk much more after that. My new medicine might not have been needed, and I'm relieved that it didn't make matters worse." Tears trickled past the wall he'd erected so far, the belief that Ian was recovering giving his emotions room to burst out, as well. "This is my fault!"

Isabeau looked at him sharply. "You aren't saying you poisoned him, after all?"

"No!" He widened his eyes with horror. "But I poured him more of the brandywine and left it by the bed when I went to gather my medicinals for the trip. If I hadn't done that, he wouldn't have drunk more and gotten as sick as he did."

"You are *not* to blame, and you most certainly are the one who saved him." When he said nothing, she leaned into his line of vision. "Ian would never fault you for his illness merely because you were being a good…wife to him." She straightened. "We must be grateful that his love of brandywine didn't make a glutton of him. He usually guzzles the stuff when he's in a festive mood. Someone must have known of his tastes."

Calan shook his head, the need for the truth coming at last now that he was beginning to hope for a happy outcome. And besides, the guard has witnessed his confrontation with Celia. Word would spread to the Moorcondians, regardless. "No. The person who poisoned it only knew that I *don't* like it, so there was no chance of my being killed along with my husband."

"What are saying?"

Before Calan could answer, there was a knock on the door. He and Isabeau turned toward it.

A guard poked her head in. "Apologies, my lady, but Councillor Fennic is insisting on speaking with you...and the countess," she added with a glance at Calan.

Instead of answering the guard, Isabeau looked at Calan. "What is your wish? Ian is your husband, after all, and this your room."

Perhaps he shouldn't have been, given how the woman had acted that morning, but Calan was once again surprised by her deference. He slipped off the bed and said, "Let him in."

Fennic stepped inside, wringing his hands and his gaze whirling around the room. As it landed on Ian, his face drained of color. "H-how fairs the count?"

"He is improving," Calan replied. "Lady Isabeau and I are guardedly hopeful that he will recover."

Fennic's head bobbed a few times. "Excellent news. We have all been most anxious about his condition. Little information has come forward, so we feared the worse."

"He was poisoned." Calan stated the bare fact baldly, his anger replacing his fear.

"Yes." Fennic didn't hold his gaze. "So I understand. And that is why I have come." He turned his attention to Isabeau. "My lady, there have been...suggestions that you were responsible."

Ian's sister gasped. "Is that what you think?" she demanded of Calan.

He shook his head. "No. I'm sure you didn't, actually."

"Then who has put that vicious rumor about?"

"The person who actually did the deed — Aunt Celia." Calan rubbed his chest over his heart because facing this awful truth hurt.

Fennic wrung his hands even more. "Oh, dear. This is very bad business, indeed. It is known, my lady, that you disapproved of your brother's marriage to Calan." His eyes were almost pleading, as if he were doing a terrible duty and wanted to be wrong—which he was, but through no fault of his own.

Calan responded before Isabeau could. "The idea that Lady Isabeau would try to kill her own brother along with me is absurd, if you think hard about it. Not only is her love for him obvious to all who care to observe, but it would also have made far more sense for her to wait until we returned to Moorcondia before getting rid of me—after securing the formula from me, of course. That way, she'd have the treaty and free Ian to marry a suitable woman. Surely you don't believe this woman is stupid."

Fennic's eyes popped. "No, no, of course not. It's just—"

"My Aunt Celia has spun some tale that sounded plausible when she told it, but now you see how implausible it actually is."

Lady Isabeau found her voice. "It was her, your aunt? You're sure?"

Calan closed his eyes briefly, the painful truth overwhelming for a moment. He opened his eyes and stared at Fennic only. He was the one who had to be convinced. "Yes. When I saw her in the workshop early this morning, she spoke as if she knew what had happened. That's why I raced back here as I did. She implicated Lady Isabeau and indicating that while she knew of what had happened, she had decided it was best not to interfere. That was clever of her," he allowed. "But I'm sure that's not what happened. Aunt Celia obtained a bottle of brandywine to poison because, although she couldn't know for sure that Ian would drink it, she was certain I wouldn't touch it. With Ian dead, she would have me back in her control.

"I saw her again a short while ago when I went to retrieve what I hoped would be the antidote. She barged in and continued to deny her culpability." He paused before daring to say out loud what had been torturing his mind for hours now. "I think I saw a hint of madness in her eyes. She's always been volatile behind closed doors, but this was more than the anger she's unleashed on me over the years. Taking this horrid step and thinking she could get away with it is not the act of a rational person. Apparently, she will do anything to achieve what she is convinced is right—keeping me as a useful tool for Shadow Valley alone. And for her benefit, as well," he added with sadness. The bright woman who had taught him so much seemed intent on stealing his ideas for herself.

"I don't follow the logic, dear boy," Fennic said. "The death of the count would change nothing. You would still have had the right to move to Moorcondia as the widowed countess and the treaty—"

"Oh, you would have torn that up, would you not?" Isabeau interjected.

Calan nodded. "Yes. If you thought Lady Isabeau had killed her brother and tried to kill me, the council wouldn't have gone through with the treaty. Such evil is not tolerated in Shadow Valley, and no one would want to have anything to do with a country that fostered such a thing. Aunt Celia could keep me and the secret of the cordial here."

Fennic went over to a chair and sat heavily. "If that is true, you are describing a vile plan that I can't imagine of your aunt."

"You know her, Councillor Fennic." Calan went to stand in front of him. "She's always been controlling, and her feelings about the treaty were no secret. And I've been on the receiving end of her temper, something that she and I both hid from the rest of you. Me, out of shame and a sense of loyalty to my own family. She's been clever enough to keep the worst of her impulses in check around others. As much as it pains me to say it, this act doesn't surprise me. Not really."

"What are we to do?"

"I would ask that you do nothing for the moment. What matters to me is Ian's recovery. After that… Well, I'm not on the council, am I? It's not my decision."

Fennic opened his mouth, but before he had a chance to speak, there was a low moan from the bed.

Calan whipped his head around and practically leaped to his husband's side. "Ian? Can you hear me?"

A ghost of a smile graced the man's face. "Darling." That one word was said in a whisper, and Ian's eyes remained close. It didn't matter. This was wonderful progress.

Calan grinned at Isabeau. "I think he's going to recover."

She put an arm around Calan and hugged him briefly. "Of course, he is…thanks to you. I cannot tell you how sorry I am that I fought this marriage. If I hadn't been so openly hostile, your aunt might not have believed her scheme would work. I must shoulder some of the blame."

Calan shook his head. "No. Ian won't think so, any more than he'd castigate me for unwittingly giving him more of the poison. You were right about that, and please accept that I'm right about this."

Isabeau gave him a good, hard stare as she stepped back. "I can see now why Ian was drawn to you from the beginning. It's not only your outward beauty. There is great goodness in you. And you are obviously happy with each other, and that's all that truly matters."

Fennic hovered a little way away. "Countess, my lady, what would you have me do?"

At Isabeau's nod for him to answer, Calan said, "Nothing...for now. Speak of my husband's recovery to no one. Let Celia think he's still in danger. When he's well, Ian will know what should be done — or at least he'll undoubtedly have very strong ideas." He gazed down at Ian, who seemed to be sleeping more than unconscious. "I suspect he always does."

* * * *

The murmuring around Ian started to sound clearer. Gone was the ringing in his ears, and his body no longer felt as if it were on fire. He took in a deep breath, free from the constricting pain that had made him scream inside his own head. He'd tried to open his eyes and mouth before, but nothing had worked. Now, he knew that while it would be hard to do so, he'd succeed. He pried open his eyelids. The first thing in his line of vision was his wife. *Of course.*

He managed a smile. "Darling Calan."

The boy's eyes popped, and he uttered a gasp before leaning into him. "You're awake. Truly this time."

This time? Obviously Ian's memories of what had been going on were murky. "Have I been away for very long?"

"A few days." Tears filled Calan's eyes.

Ian tried to lift his hand to wipe them away, but it was too hard. It dropped back onto the bed like a stone. "How very inconsiderate of me to worry you so." He licked his dry, cracked lips. "Might I have some water, wife?"

Calan jumped to comply, filling a cup from a pitcher by the bed. When the boy tried to lift him up enough to drink, a second set of arms helped from the other side. "Sister?" He didn't say anything more as he concentrated all his energy—of which there was disconcertingly little—to sip the cool liquid. Nothing had ever tasted so good.

When he was done, his wife and sister propped him against a mound of pillows.

Calan's worried face entered his line of sight once more. "How do you feel?"

"Weak as a kitten. I don't like it," he added with a petulant tone that he also didn't like yet couldn't quite hold back. "Have I been sick?" Alarm shot through him suddenly. "Were you?" He tried once more to touch Calan, although this time, to make sure the boy was well.

Calan intercepted his hand and held it in his lap. "I'm fine. I didn't drink any of the brandywine."

Ian frowned. "Drink... It was poisoned?" Fury helped clear his fuzzy head.

Calan nodded. "I'm afraid so."

"Your aunt." He didn't need to ask, because he *knew* with instant and obvious clarity.

His wife looked surprised, however. "How did you guess?"

"A logical deduction, darling. She never tried to hide her hatred of me, and who else would have the skill or the motive to do so? Other than Isabeau, of course, but she isn't the kind to poison. If she wanted me dead, she'd take a dagger to my heart." He managed to shoot his sister a smile. "And your aunt would know, would she not, that you don't drink brandywine?"

Calan nodded his head, misery written across his face. "Yes, you're right, although she has tried to blame Lady Isabeau."

Now, Ian struggled to sit up, a bold move fueled by his anger, but ultimately fruitless, given his weakened state. He flopped immediately back onto the pillows. "How dare she. That…" He didn't finish his thought, sensitive to the fact that the woman was his wife's only relative.

Calan placed his hand on Ian's chest. "Please don't upset yourself or try to do too much. Your recovery is going to take a few more days. And there is nothing you can call Celia or say about her that I'll disagree with." He lowered his gaze. "I still can't believe she'd do such a thing. I guess I didn't realize how much she wanted to keep and control me, and you nearly died because of my failure." Tears trickled down his cheeks.

Ian used what little strength he had to do the most important thing at the moment. Reaching up, he wiped away those tears from Calan's cheek before exhaustion overtook him once more. "Please don't cry, darling. You are not to blame for any of this. I knew of her feelings and should have been more vigilant." Just thinking of how he'd almost tried to persuade the boy to drink some of the brandywine chilled his blood.

"Indeed, you should have been." Isabeau entered his line of sight. "It's a good thing that your wife is a brilliant apothecary. His latest innovation saved you. You have chosen well in your marriage, brother." She gave him a brief smile, reminding him of how beautiful she was and how little there was for her to be happy about, other than Amalie, since her husband's death.

"Does this mean you approve of my marriage now, sister?"

She lifted her chin, her haughtiness back on display. "How could I not be, given your wife's obvious love for you?"

"Love?" Ian shot his gaze over to Calan. The boy was back to blushing with adorable embarrassment, a wonderful difference than his pale-faced worry of a moment before. And as much as Ian enjoyed his wife's pretty pink face, he understood that the boy had been through an ordeal, thanks to him, however inadvertently. He smiled as much as his tiredness permitted. "Well, that's good to know…seeing as I love him, too."

Chapter Ten

Calan fussed with tucking Ian in after his sponge bath. "There you go. It must feel good to be clean."

It embarrassed Ian to realize just how true that was. Not since early childhood had he felt such pleasure in something as simple as having the sweat wiped off his body and having fresh sheets to lie on. And he'd never been so incapacitated since those few times in his life when sickness had claimed him with the same force as it had other children. It was annoyingly disconcerting that his dick had laid limp, despite his wife's touch. He was used to being vigorous in all ways. Being an invalid didn't suit him. *But I'm still alive, and that's what matters.*

"You are the best nursemaid I've ever had. Thank you."

Calan puttered around, folding the wet cloth and putting the bowl of dirty water by the door for someone to pick up later. "You're welcome, but you needn't keep saying things you think I want to hear. I'm your wife, and catering to you is my pleasure."

Ian understood that the boy wasn't referring to his thanks. Since that day when he'd come around fully and had confessed his love for his wife, Calan had refused to speak of that declaration head on. The silly boy seemed to believe that Ian had spoken merely out of gratitude. Nothing could be further from the truth, and while it would have been preferable for an occasion other than near death to get him to say the words, now that he had, he wasn't going to retreat from them.

"I love you, wife…even if my sorry excuse of a cock is unable to demonstrate it."

Calan rolled his eyes. "Only you would think that an inability to become aroused after a near-death illness is something to apologize for."

Ian tried to look abashed. "It's true that a significant amount of my pride resides between my legs. You are a magnificent temptation, even in my weakened state—in my mind, at least. I look forward to my speedy recovery if only so that I can show you how much I love you and not merely say the words."

"Do you feel up to trying something more solid than broth?"

Hmm, such a stubborn boy. "Yes, actually." His stomach grumbled with hunger for the first time since he'd woken.

That cheered his wife. "Good. I'll ask Isabeau to put some chicken in the soup and see how well you hold that down. She's making all your food herself, you know, with ingredients she gathers herself, too. And guards surround her at all times. There is no chance of any more poison getting into you or of her being at risk."

Ian was both surprised and not at the news. "My sister has always been one to take an active role in her homes and not merely leaving everything to servants, but as a supervisor. I had no idea she could cook."

"You shouldn't be surprised. I bet she's much like you when it comes to staying busy and being useful."

Ian frowned. "Yes, I suppose so. And as she's always teased me about being like a laborer, this means I get to give her some grief back, knowing that she is competent in the kitchen. And you keep changing the subject whenever I bring love up," he added, because he wasn't going to allow his wife to distract him.

Calan pursed his lips and twisted his fingers in front of him. "You don't need to keep professing your love to me just because Isabeau let out how I feel and you're grateful for my care."

Now Ian was a bit affronted. "Really, wife, do you not know me better than that? I'm not one to say anything I don't mean, and while I appreciate your saving my life, there are other ways of showing my gratitude than telling a lie."

Calan gazed down at his hands. "I didn't mean to imply that you were lying… Not really. It's only that I've been with recovering patients before, and it's an emotional time. Words can be said and feelings confessed that are confused with gratitude."

His wife's obvious discomfort caused Ian to change tack. "Do you love me, Calan?"

The boy's gaze flew up. "Of course, I do! Isabeau wasn't simply telling you something she thought you wanted to hear."

Calan's earnest expression and the sincerity in his eyes helped give Ian strength more than any concoction or food ever could. "That makes me ecstatically happy, darling. And I believe you mean it and aren't just saying those words because I almost died."

Calan frowned. "You're throwing my words back in my face."

"Of course, I am."

"I don't like that."

"I didn't expect that you would." Ian grinned. "I will let this topic lie for the moment, wife, if only because I'm starving all of a sudden. But we will come back to it—pretty much every day for the rest of our lives. Eventually, you'll believe me."

Calan threw up his hands. "Oh, you're an impossibly smug man."

Ian deepened his grin. "Yes, I really am. But you love me, nevertheless, and I…" He let his gaze finish his thought.

His wife didn't take the bait. "I'll get your food." He stomped out in high dungeon.

Ian sighed and let his weakness take over him. He really was the luckiest of men, the poisoning notwithstanding. And although he hated how slowly his recovery was taking, it did give him time to ponder what to do about Celia. The woman was a menace, and while he wasn't worried about her reaching him again, he feared that she would find a way to turn her ire on Calan. It was the next logical step in her mad plan—and it was insane. He hoped Calan realized that and wouldn't be tempted to trust the woman with his own safety. Ian wasn't going to let her hurt his wife. If Shadow Valley couldn't bring itself to mete out the punishment she deserved, he would see to it himself. Calan might never forgive him, no matter what the woman had done, but Ian would worry about that later. Nothing mattered more than his wife's safety.

* * * *

"Don't overdo it."

Ian stretched and lifted his face to the sun. The warmth of it as well as the fresh air was a kind of medicine in itself, nature's endless way of giving someone strength. "You worry too much, wife." He tightened his grip on Calan's hand. "I may not be a hundred percent myself yet, but I feel strong enough for a stroll." He leered at Calan. "Maybe for even more, if we find a secluded spot."

With a gasp, Calan swatted at Ian's chest. "Your sister can hear."

Ian glanced at Isabeau, who stood primly on his other side. "That's all right. She's a mother, after all, and therefore well-acquainted with what married people get up to."

"Don't tease the boy, brother. He's gotten very little sleep these many days of nursing you back to health. You'd be a better husband if you find a place for you both to take a nap, as in *sleeping*," she emphasized.

The last thing Ian wanted to do was lie down again, but his sister was right. Calan's lovely eyes had dark circles under them. He ran the fingers of his free hand down one soft cheek. "You have overtaxed yourself, darling. Let's take a blanket into the maze and rest by the fountain."

Calan's face lit up. "That's a wonderful idea."

Ian loved making the boy happy, but before he could order one of the guards to fetch a blanket, Councillor Fennic hurried over. Ian resigned himself to having a conversation that he would have preferred to put off a little longer.

"My lord, it's so good to see you up and about. When no word of your progress came forward, we feared the worst."

"My recovery has been slow, but thanks to my wife and my sister, I am quite well now—well enough to venture out." And because there was no point now in beating around the bush, he asked the obvious question. "Where is Celia?"

Fennic averted his gaze. "I know not. Around somewhere, I suppose. The council has not met since your... We wanted to wait until you were well before tackling the problem."

Calan huffed. "So you haven't even confronted her or confined her to her house?"

Fennic shrugged. "You should know better than your husband, Countess, that Shadow Valley doesn't have much in the way of crime, let alone attempted murder." He focused again on Ian. "We usually force some kind of restitution for matters such as theft. For more violent matters, because we have no prisons, we use banishment."

Ian lifted an eyebrow. "Making the guilty party someone else's problem."

Fennic had the good grace to look embarrassed. "Just so. Your...guidance in this would be greatly appreciated."

"I will handle it. Rest assured, Councillor."

The man's relief was obvious. "Thank you, My Lord. We won't question your decision or how you decide to mete out justice." With a bow, he raced away.

Calan opened his mouth, but Ian overrode whatever objection he was sure the boy intended to make. "We'll talk about Celia later. For now, let's enjoy the day."

"Are you sure you'll be safe?"

Ian gestured to the guards standing around them. "Quite sure." Because he would never take a risk with his wife's life, but he wasn't going to add that point.

Calan didn't appreciate his value...not yet. Ian would change that—and soon. "And as we'll have no privacy anyway, we may as well make it a picnic." He looked at Isabeau. "Would you and Amalie care to join us?"

"Of course. As you say, we'll be perfectly safe, and we've been cooped up here as much as you have."

That settled that. Ian waited as patiently as he could manage for his sister to make the arrangements. He contented himself with gazing upon his wife, admiring his beauty and taking comfort in planning exactly what he would do to and with the boy once he was back to full strength. Happily, his cock stirred ever so slightly at such thoughts, testament that he was on the mend.

Eventually, they were off, guards ahead, behind and flanking them, Ian leading the way from the middle with Calan firmly in hand. Isabeau walked behind them with Amalie and her nursemaid, except the little girl danced around, despite her mother's efforts to hold on to her.

As they reached the topiary, Amalie grabbed Calan's free hand. "Uncle Calan, will you please make shrub animals for me at Truehart Manor?"

Calan glanced at Ian before answering. "Of course, if your mother approves."

"Oh, she will. She already said yes, so long as you were willing. And a maze! We must have one of those, too."

Calan chuckled. "Again, if your mother permits. They are fun."

"And we'll do the same at Charteris. After all, I'm going to be countess one day, so I should have a say over it now, don't you think?"

Now, Calan shot a look of alarm at Ian. "I was already planning something for there, although I haven't had a chance to discuss it with your uncle."

Ian reached around his wife's back and tugged at one of Amalie's braids. "You are becoming a hard task mistress. That being said, yes, we will start on a maze as soon as we return. I'm sure it takes many years to fully form. You'll have to be patient. I'm not sure that's your best quality."

His niece looked affronted, looking just like her mother. "Yes, it is—like with you and mama." The child skipped ahead, the guards reforming to keep her encircled.

Ian started to laugh, then caught a flash of movement at the entrance to the maze. "Stop the child!" The guards acted immediately, one of them not only grabbing Amalie, but picking her up bodily and carrying her to Lady Isabeau. "Take them both back to the house."

"Take Mistress Amalie," Isabeau corrected to the guards. "I'm with you, brother, whether you like it or not."

Calan tugged at his hand. "What is it?"

"Your aunt." He grimaced at his wife. "She just entered the maze."

"How did she know we were headed there?"

"She may not have. I don't suppose there's any point in my ordering you to go with Amalie?" His wife simply glared at him. "No, of course not. Stay by my side and do as I say without question once we catch up with her. This I must insist on."

"I understand." The boy's eyes got misty. "I don't want to be a distraction to you by making you worried about me."

Ian nodded. "Thank you." Letting go of his wife's hand, he pushed his way past the guards. "Stay behind me. Lady Isabeau and Countess Calan are your priority," he shouted to the guards.

He led the way into the maze, scanning to see which direction the woman might have gone. It was a fairly complex layout and he hadn't been through it all. Still, logic dictated that no matter what the woman's intent was, she was likely going to the center. He started down the one path he knew that led to there.

The turns came quickly, and Ian kept his stride brisk in the hope of catching up to the shorter woman. She hadn't been running when he'd caught sight of her, and he didn't hear any pounding footfalls. The sheer difference in their leg lengths should allow him to close the gap between them soon. And he was rewarded when rounding a hedgerow, he saw a flap of dress taking the next turn. He gestured toward the guards to keep up as he increased his speed.

When he reached an intersection, he turned in the direction he knew would lead to the center. Before he took two steps, Calan pulled up to his side and stopped him.

He gestured in the opposite direction. "This way. It's less well-known and takes longer to reach the center. She's using it to evade us, I'm sure, and there's nowhere else for her to go other than the fountain at this point. There are no exits, except the ones she'll have to reach by going through the center to the other side."

Ian didn't hesitate to trust his wife's judgment, and it didn't take long for him to catch another glimpse of the woman. He didn't try too hard now to overtake her. Surely Celia was aware that they followed, if she took a lesser-known route. And they weren't trying to be quiet about it, either. He took the time to consider what he was going to do once he caught her. Although he'd hoped the council would take care of matters in whatever way they had here in Shadow Valley, it was clear now that all they had was banishment. And he wasn't about to let the woman freely roam Moorcondia to seek out Calan, nor would he unleash her onto other unsuspecting countries. The best solution might be to bring her back to the king's court and let him deal with her. There would be a risk to carting her with them, but he had to consider Calan's feelings. He wasn't going to want to stand by as Ian dispatched his aunt, no matter what she'd done. This was the woman who'd raised him, after all. *I can't let him be a witness.*

His thoughts were getting ahead of his feet, however. The woman still eluded them. As they approached a corner past which Ian could both see and hear the fountain, he slowed and pushed Calan behind him. Thank the gods, the boy didn't fight him on that. He stepped out into the clearing. Celia stood by the fountain, her back straight, her gaze fixed on him. She was clearly waiting for them to arrive.

"You have led us a merry chase, madam, and muddied the waters as best you could over my poisoning. You have failed on all accounts, however. It is time for you to face the consequences." He got closer, then stopped when she held up a flask.

"You think you have me?" She shook her head. "You stole my nephew and my greatest discovery. I'm not going to let you take my life, too."

Ian kept a sharp eye on that flask. He couldn't be sure it didn't contain something explosive. "Calan developed the cordial, not you, and he never *belonged* to you, so I couldn't steal him away. He came to me freely, a fact that I shall forever be grateful for."

"Because, like every man, he thought with his dick." She sneered and looked past Ian's shoulder.

He didn't have to check to know his wife hadn't stayed put. "Please leave, darling. We don't know what she's intending to do."

"I know." Calan stepped to his side. "That flask doesn't contain anything that can harm us, only her. Isn't that right, Aunt Celia?"

"Always a bright boy." Celia took a visibly deep breath. "I could have found someone to satisfy your lust. You didn't have to get in bed with the enemy."

"Ian is not that. He never was. And I love him."

Celia's face twisted with rage. "Love! You don't know what that is. You have always been a foolish boy, better suited to daydreaming than serving our people. The proof of it is how you are taking the most valuable thing we have and handing it over to others for the price of your pleasure. You *disgust* me!"

Calan flinched as if he'd been slapped, and the way he raised a hand to his cheek confirmed that he had been before—likely many times.

"That's enough!" Ian roared and strode toward the woman, determined to take her prisoner and get her away from Calan for good.

Before he reached her, however, she unstopped the flask and drank from it. Her face screwed up in agony before she dropped to the ground. Calan flew past him and threw himself onto his knees beside her. He tried to take her in his arms, but she used what little strength she had to twist away. She convulsed a few times, then gasped as frothy pink liquid spilled from her mouth. Then...nothing.

Ian joined his wife on his knees and wrapped his arms around him, not entirely sure of his welcome. He needn't have worried. Calan pressed into him, putting his forehead against Ian's chest and wept—quietly but at length, his slender body shuddering with his sobs. When he judged that the storm was abating, Ian picked him up and carried him out of the maze. The boy had seen enough. Ian was determined to put them both to bed and rest from the ordeal. And if his legs were a little shaky on the journey back to their room, he ignored it. He wouldn't hand his wife over to anyone at that moment.

Isabeau must have noticed his weakness and didn't ignore it. She hurried to keep up with him. "Ian—"

He shushed her with a quick shake of his head.

"I'll bring lunch to your room, if you'd like. And…see to everything else."

He didn't have to ask what she meant. "Thank you."

Calan said nothing, curled up in his arms, limp. As soon as Ian laid him down on the bed, however, the boy clutched his tunic, forcing him to lie next to him.

Ian didn't have to be convinced. This was the only place he wanted to be at the moment. He rubbed the palm of his hand down Calan's back. "It's all right, darling. There was nothing you could have done to cause a different outcome."

His wife sniffed. "I know. She took control of her ending, and I can't say I'm sorry she did. I worried about your being forced to deal with her. That wouldn't have been fair to you, not that I would have held any decision you made against you. She did try to kill you, after all."

Ian shouldn't have been surprised that his wife had been in step with this thinking all along. He kissed the boy's head. "Darling, I only ever worried about you. Her madness would have caused her to turn against you if she'd been allowed to remain free. I could never have taken that chance, but she did the right thing in the end, so no need to fret over it anymore."

"No, I won't look back, but as her only kin, I must see to her funeral rights and settle her estate, such as it is. It will mean staying here longer and filling at least one wagon with the furniture and other mementos of my family I'll want to keep now that she doesn't own them."

"Of course, darling, whatever you need." There was a knock on the door. "Here's Isabeau with our luncheon. Do you feel up to eating?"

Calan pulled out of his arms in order to look him in the eye. "As long as you're by my side, I can handle anything."

* * * *

When Calan's parents had died, he'd been too young to send them off in the proper way. Celia had done it for him. As her only remaining family, it fell to him to honor the Shadow Valley funeral rights. It didn't matter what the woman had done in life. There were customs to be observed for his own sake and that of their community as much as anything she desired. So, he went into proper mourning, cladding himself in black and rending the collar of his tunic to demonstrate his grief. Ian and Isabeau caused him to tear up when they followed suit, even though it was nothing they were used to. They didn't even ask the why of it, simply followed his example. They even helped him cover all the mirrors in their rooms and sat all day with him as people came to express their condolences. No one mentioned Celia's perfidy or the fact that she had ended her own life — something their culture frowned upon.

Calan was beyond grateful for all the support. And as he walked past the crowd gathered at the funeral site, torch in hand, he kept his head high. There were no tears, though. He'd shed what he had in him right after her death. Now, even though he did his duty to her, he couldn't forgive his aunt for trying to kill his husband. Madness it might have been, but he knew she understood very clearly what she was doing. He'd seen clarity in her gaze that last time they'd spoken in the workshop. What she'd done had been calculated, and she'd shown no regret before downing the poison that had killed her quickly, if not quite painlessly. She hadn't given Ian that consideration. Whatever she'd used, it had been meant to kill Ian slowly and agonizingly.

He stopped in front of the pyre where Celia's body lay wrapped tightly in a white shroud. Isabeau had taken over the chore of seeing to the preparation without being asked. He owed her so much for that gesture and for trusting him to take care of Ian. She stood beside her brother, and Calan shot a quick smile at them both before turning back to his task. He stuck the torch into the kindling underneath the pyre and stepped away as the flames caught quickly.

The heat of the fire started to rob him of his breath and still he remained standing there, watching what was left of his family burn. That was the wrong way of thinking of his life, though. Ian reminded him that he still had a family — a new and loving one — by coming to him and pulling him into his arms and away from the flames. Calan clung to his husband and leaned on the strength of his embrace as he watched until there was nothing more than ashes. Once they cooled down, villagers would come and take some to mix in with fertilizer for fields and gardens. In this way, the departed helped renew life for those left behind. He wouldn't be gathering any. There was a new life waiting for him in Moorcondia and given recent events, he wanted to take only those things that mattered to him.

Ian squeezed his shoulders. "Shall we leave now?"

"Yes." Calan allowed his husband to steer him away. "There's one ritual left to observe, if that's okay?"

"Certainly, darling. You must mourn your aunt in whatever way pleases you. I'm not going to leave your side, either."

"Thank you and it's not anything burdensome. There's a special cake for us to eat and wine to drink back in our room. We're supposed to raise a glass to Aunt Celia's memory, but I don't really want to do that. I've given her what I could, and there's nothing more left in me."

"You've been a dutiful nephew, Calan. No one can ask more of you."

He said nothing more as they walked, emotion forming a lump in his throat. It wasn't grief, but love that did so. Being Ian's wife, living the rest of his days with this man, was more than he'd ever hoped for. He was determined to make the most out of the gift the gods had given him.

Back in the room, he made short work of his final gesture to his aunt. He poured two glasses of sweet wine and broke off two pieces of the small, dense cake that had been left at his request and handed one of each to Ian. Saying nothing, he took a bite of his cake and a sip of his wine. His husband did the same, and when Calan put the rest down, so did Ian.

"Is that all that needs to be done?"

Calan nodded. "Yes, the cake is too dry and the wine too cloying for my tastes. I don't think anyone enjoys them, to be honest." He glanced at the bed and gnawed at his lower lip. "How are you feeling?"

His husband got a gleam in his eyes. "Fully recovered, wife. Why do you ask?"

Calan held out his hand, understanding Ian knew only too well why. "Take me to bed."

* * * *

Calan felt no guilt over letting Ian take control. It was a blessed relief to let go of the stress of the last few days and allow his husband to play with his body however he wished. First, Ian undressed him, then pulled back the sheets to lay Calan naked and already flushed with the first heat of passion onto the cool bedding. His cock was achingly hard. They hadn't made love since that horrid night of the poisoning. He was beyond ready to be ravished into oblivion. And the way his husband's hungry gaze roamed over him as he quickly shed his own clothes made him shudder with anticipation.

Ian grabbed the pot of cream that Calan had made sure was handy and pouring some into his palm, slicking his hard dick. "I'm sorry, darling, but it's been too long. This first time is going to be more rushed than I would like."

Calan closed his eyes to half-mast and groaned, bucking his hip as he did so. "I want it that way. Fuck me, Ian, hard and fast. Don't hold anything back."

"Never with you."

His husband crawled onto the bed, still gripping the pot, and nudged Calan's legs apart with his knee. Calan didn't need to be told what to do. He bent his knees, holding his legs open by clasping the underneath of his thighs. When Ian slipped two coated fingers into his hole, Calan clenched around them and moaned loudly. Ian thrust a few times and twisted his fingers around to loosen the puckered ring. Then he scraped across Calan's prostate, making him moan and thrash. He mewled in disappointment when his husband pulled his fingers out. That was only a moment of disappointment, of course, because Ian came back immediately with something larger and more satisfying. As his man filled Calan's ass with one long slide, Calan's first orgasm ripped through him.

He came with a wildness that forced his eyelids to slam down, and he dug his fingertips into the flesh of his own thighs. The bite of pain only added to the intensity of the climax, as did the burn of being breached so quickly. He liked it this way. It made him feel marked and confirmed his husband's mastery over him. He wanted more — of everything.

Letting go of his thighs, he held out his hands. "Come here. Kiss me."

Ian wasted no time, bracing himself over Calan and claiming his lips in a bruising kiss. He fucked Calan's mouth as he fucked his ass, with long, fast strokes. Calan gripped his husband's shoulders, and wrapping his legs around the man's hips, bounced his heels against his ass to urge him to greater speed. Ian heeded the demand, rolling his hips to slap his pelvis against Calan's backside, driving his dick deeper inside. With a roar, he came, his cum flooding Calan and causing him to orgasm again. And still the man fucked him, his cock pressing against Calan's swollen channel. He vaguely thought Ian would slow down, but he was wrong. His husband only stopped thrusting into him after they both climaxed once again.

When it was over, Calan dropped both his arms and legs, wrung dry and limp. Ian collapsed on top of him, his heavy weight pressing Calan into the mattress. He loved the feeling of his husband covering him, even if it was a little hard to breathe. Always attuned to Calan's needs, Ian rolled off him and gathered him in his arms.

"Thank you, darling. I quite needed that."

Calan laughed. "The master of understatement— and why do you always act as if I'm doing you a favor when we have sex?"

"Make love," Ian gently corrected. "And because you are still a marvel to me, dear wife. I can scarcely believe that you are mine." He paused for a few seconds. "I love you."

As he had the other times his husband had said those words, Calan started to dismiss them as merely a reassurance his husband thought he needed to give. But he didn't say anything out loud. Not immediately. He gave himself permission to sit with the declaration and consider that Ian meant it, that he truly loved him. "I want you to…love me, that is." After everything that had happened, he found the courage to make himself vulnerable. If he didn't trust his husband with his feelings, what chance did they have for a happy marriage?

Ian leaned away and lifted Calan's head up a gently tug of his hair. "Good. Because I do—love you, Calan. I'm not merely saying what I think you want to hear. I mean it and have each time I've said it. Why is that so hard for you to believe?"

Calan opened his mouth, then shut it again with a frown. "I don't know. Maybe because I've always had a vision of a powerful man like you not succumbing to the fragility of loving someone."

Ian raised his eyebrows. "Falling in love takes courage, my dear, and strength. Giving your heart to someone is not a sign of weakness. And when the person whom you love is as amazing and generous and loving as you are?" He shrugged. "How could I *not* fall in love with you?"

Well, when you put it that *way*. Calan smiled. "I guess I've been afraid. I guess it's hard for me to appreciate my appeal. I'm nothing special."

Ian smacked his butt lightly. "Never say that again!"

Startled by the admonishment, Calan stared at his husband with wide eyes. "Okay."

Ian gathered him close again. "Darling, you are driving me to distraction. I love you, and if I have to spend the rest of our lives convincing you of that fact and that you are worthy of any man's love, I shall do so. Never underestimate me."

"I won't," Calan assured him, his face mashed against the man's hard chest. "I love you, too."

"Naturally. Now," he added rolling Calan onto his stomach, "let me kiss your poor ass where I hit it."

"You don't... Oh." His husband didn't end with a simple kiss. He started with one, then licked his way down to lap at Calan's balls.

The man had a wicked tongue on him. He knew just how to employ it to raise Calan's passion once more. He squeaked with surprise when Ian used his large hands to part the globes of Calan's ass. He blew against the puckered ring, sending a delightful tingle up Calan's spine. But it was the use of that tongue again that drove Calan wild. It should have been embarrassing to have his husband lick his hole. Such an intimate act. The gentle lapping caused him to relax and open up so that he was more than ready for Ian's cock as he slid it in.

This fucking was long and slow. With two orgasms under his belt, Ian was in no hurry. The man was a marvel to be hard again so soon. Calan allowed himself to just lie there and enjoy the steady rocking of Ian's hips against his ass. His hard yet sensitive dick was rubbing against the sheet. It was almost too much. *Almost.* He came again with a sigh and saying Ian's name in a whisper. Then he fell blissfully asleep as his husband continued to fuck him.

* * * *

Calan stood in his empty workshop and took one last look around. It was hard to believe he was really leaving. The house was empty, ready for its new owners to move their own things in. The newly married couple had been overjoyed at his gifting of it to them. He didn't need the money. Being the Countess of Charteris meant he had a pile of it all to himself — or so Isabeau had assured him and that was even so not counting the revenue he'd receive from the sale of the cordial. Besides, he liked the idea of a new family starting out here and making it into a happy place. It had never been that for him. He could admit that sad fact now that his aunt was gone, and he was heading to a better life.

Ian stepped into the doorway. "The wagons are all packed, darling. You've managed to fill both of them to the brim."

Calan scraped his teeth over his top lip. "Did I keep too much?"

"Of course not." His husband came over and hugged him. "I'm only teasing. I'd gladly buy a hundred more wagons if there were more you want to bring."

Calan rolled his eyes as he held him close. "No, thank you. I have everything I need and want, mostly because it's standing in front of me," he added pulling away. "I didn't expect to take much more than the clothes on my back when I agreed to marry you. Thank you for giving me the extra time to sort all of this out."

"Calan, I will give you whatever is in my power to. I love you."

"And I love you." Since the night of the funeral, they'd taken to saying those words to each other every day at least once. It had become a kind of game to see who thought of declaring their love first.

"Well, now that's settled — again. Shall we go?" Ian held out his hand.

Taking it, Calan said, "May I ask for one more favor today?"

"Of course." Ian squeezed his hand.

"I'd like my last look at Shadow Valley as we leave to be the first one you had — by the lake. Do you remember?"

Ian chuckled. "The vision of you right before you dove into the water is seared into my brain, darling."

He pulled Calan's hand up to kiss it. "I know just where to stop."

* * * *

The Charteris carriage was a lot smaller on the inside with Ian's large body folded into it. Calan didn't mind. It meant he had the perfect excuse to cuddle up against his husband. And having Lady Isabeau and Amalie riding with them made the journey more pleasant. The little girl chattered incessantly with excitement. Calan liked it because it helped pass the time and distracted him from his nervousness over leaving his homeland. He had no doubts whatsoever about the turn his life was taking. It was still hard not to feel sad at the thought he might never see Shadow Valley again.

Ian rapped suddenly on the roof of the carriage. "We are here, darling." To Isabeau, he said, "This is the same spot where we stopped to stretch our legs on the journey here. I want to show Calan something."

Amalie bounced. "Oh, can I come too?"

Her mother shook her head before Ian could respond. "Certainly not. Your uncles need a private moment. We'll go see your nurse, and you may tend to any needs you might have."

The child wasn't happy at that answer, but she made no complaint as they all left the carriage and followed her mother with only one backward glance.

Calan took a moment to breathe in the air he knew so well. When Ian put his arm around him and led them into the forest, he went with muted excitement. He loved the lake and wanted not only one last look at it, but he also wanted to see it as Ian had so many days before. A great deal had happened since. It seemed as if a lifetime had gone by.

As they reached the spot, Ian stopped and pulled him closer. "Here is where I saw you. Up on the rock." He pointed to the topmost part of the outcrop where Calan had always dove from. It was strange to see it from this vantage point.

"What did you think of me?" he dared to ask.

"I thought you were a woodland creature, a fairy from my childhood tales come alive—the most exquisite creature I'd ever laid eyes on," he added, hugging him even closer.

Calan melted against his husband's chest. "You must have been disappointed to find out I'm only an ordinary boy."

Ian chuckled. "A boy, yes, but never ordinary. And besides, if you had been a mythical being, I wouldn't have been able to marry you and have you for the rest of my life." He sighed. "I have never been happier to be so wrong."

Something lifted from Calan's heart, the last vestiges of any doubt he had about leaving his childhood home melted away. With a man such as Ian loving him, only good things could happen from now on.

He stood on tiptoes to give Ian a too-chaste kiss with the promise of more to come. "Take me home, husband. I'm ready."

Epilogue

"Darling, you are fiendishly clever. This maze is far bigger and more complicated than I expected in such a short time." Ian laughed as his wife tugged him this way and that, taking dizzying turns around the hedgerows.

Calan laughed too. "You said I could do whatever I liked."

"So I did." The transition from living in Shadow Valley to becoming a Moorcondian had been smoother for the boy than Ian had feared. Calan was resilient, more than he'd realized. And the fact that everyone on the estate obviously liked and respected him was a help. That reaction by his people to being introduced to his male bride hadn't surprised him. How could anyone know Calan and not love him? The past year had been blissful, and the development and distribution of the cordial was already making a big difference to his people's lives.

"We're almost to the center." Calan picked up speed as he said so.

Ian let himself be pulled into the middle of the maze. There was a large, elaborate fountain, just as they'd planned. Ian was pleased to see for the first time that his engineers had succeeded in making it work. It was a beautiful spot, and he looked forward to spending a lot of time there — with his wife.

Calan stopped short and rounded on him. "Hey, how did that get here?" He pointed to the wide hammock spread by four ornate rods planted deep in the grassy ground.

Ian couldn't keep the grin off his face. "Oh that? Well, I have my ways, darling. This was always part of my plan for the maze. I just wanted to surprise you." He scooped his wife into his arms and marched over to the hammock. He sat gingerly, testing the security of the moorings. Finding it sufficient, he rolled them both onto the swaying cloth.

Calan clutched at him, giggling. "Are we supposed to nap here?"

"Yes. After I've ravaged you, naturally." He covered his wife and kissed him soundly.

Once he let Calan come up for air, the boy eyed him. "And how are we supposed to do that while this thing swings us back and forth?"

He kissed him again, lightly this time. "With love."

Want to see more from this author? Here's a taster for you to enjoy!

Treaty Brides: The Desert Bride
Samantha Cayto

Excerpt

Sir Geoffrey Arbuthnott gazed around at the relentlessly barren landscape and sighed. "You know, Lucas, it's times like these that make me truly wish to have been born my parents' third son. The thought of living in a quiet monastery brewing ale has great appeal."

His right-hand man snorted. "No, you don't. Beer-making is only part of your brother's life, and I can't imagine you kneeling on a stone floor in endless prayer. And before you run through your other brotherly options, you would hate farming, politicking and commerce just as much. Being a soldier suits you best, old friend."

Geoffrey watched the king's cartographer, Professor Johns, jump off his wagon seat with surprising alacrity for a man of his age and physique. And he did so while holding a pad of paper and pencil, no less. The man squinted into the distance before sketching furiously.

Geoff suppressed another sigh. "Except this isn't soldiering."

"It could be. Not that it looks like anyone lives in this arid place. I mean, where would they find enough water to drink and to grow food?"

The question highlighted their own predicament. Since entering this desert area far to the west of Moorcondia, he'd implemented strict rationing of their supplies. There was a real possibility that they'd have to turn back soon if they didn't find natural springs to replenish their canteens and flora and fauna to cull for more food. If that happened, it would mean failing, and he'd never done that in his life. Boring this mission may be, but he was determined to make it a success.

"We've seen enough rodents scurrying about, and we'll eat those if nothing else presents itself. The gods know we've dined on worse during our campaigns. There must be sources of water. It's a matter of finding them, that's all." He scanned the skies, and his heart ticked up a beat at the sight of some birds circling in the distance. There." He pointed. "We go in that direction."

Lucas squinted up. "Hmm. Could be promising." He issued a sharp whistle to gain the attention of the other soldiers and waved in the direction they would head.

Once the cartographer had returned to his seat on the wagon, they resumed their journey. They'd traded their warhorses for stout working ones. The beasts weren't made for speed, but they were perfect for plodding along all day. And they'd brought replacements that carried provisions. If worse came to worst, they could always use them as sources of food, although he hated the idea. Previous scouts had warned them of this desert, so they had prepared as best they could. The problem was no one knew how large this area of the world was—and what, if anything other than perhaps ocean, lay on the other side. It was possible it was so vast they'd have to turn around and try again with even more supplies. The idea was depressing. He was a soldier, not an explorer, but with the Marshers subdued and the danger of the Swarm neutralized, his skills were in low demand. A good thing for Moorcondia. A bad thing for someone who'd spent his entire manhood training and fighting.

Geoff kept his gaze on the large birds flying in tight circles up ahead. They were scavengers, he was sure of it, although nothing he'd seen before. The cartographer was a good hand at drawing, as his profession demanded, and the man was memorializing everything he saw. Someone, someday, back in Moorcondia, would give names to every bit of scrub and creature they came across. That part was not his job. He and his men were there to protect Professor Johns. So far, it had been an easy task. The man was eccentric, to be sure, but he was also affable — and seemingly fearless. A recently widowed man, he'd professed a keen desire to make a mark for the remainder of his life, regardless of the risk. One couldn't help but admire the man.

It was hard to judge distance in this environment. What had looked far away proved to be closer. They hadn't gone far before Geoff was delighted to spy some greenery — or at least plants that were less brown than what they'd seen so far. It had to mean a source of water. There was a palpable sense of excitement in his men, although they were too well trained to prod their horses to a greater speed. Conservation of energy was critical, and where there was water, there could be dangerous animals — the human kind, most of all. When they were close enough to make out more detail, Geoff held up his hand to stop the procession.

He signaled two men to go with him while giving Lucas the order to stay put with the professor and the others. Then he proceeded at the same cautious speed, keeping his eyes fixed on his destination. He took in each detail as they came into focus. It was indeed a large oasis with a wide shimmering pool of water, tall thin trees with leavy greens at the top and…a horse. He stopped and blinked against the glare of the sun to be sure he was seeing correctly. And yes, it was a short, stout dappled horse with only a blanket thrown over its back. It stood to one side of the spot, grazing on some kind of low-lying shrubbery. It didn't appear to be injured or sick, so the scavengers hadn't been drawn by this animal. Not far from it, there was a dark blob seeming to float within the sand just beyond the water. A few steps later, he realized it wasn't bits of carrion as he'd expected, but a head — a human one.

Now he kicked his mount into a fast trot, still scanning the horizon for danger. He slowed again once he'd reached the oasis, skirting the water as he headed for whoever was trapped in the sand. Relief washed over him when the head of hair and the arms attached to the same body moved. Whoever this was, they were alive. As he rounded to the front of the person, his breath caught at the sight of who was in trouble. Geoff hadn't had any discernible expectations of who he'd find, but this vision caught him by surprise, nevertheless. It was a young man, hardly out of boyhood, with coppery skin and long straight hair, black as night and plaited on both sides. He looked up at him with wide dark-brown eyes.

Reining his horse to a stop, Geoff tried for a reassuring smile. "Don't worry. I'll get you out of there." When the boy didn't respond, he wondered if he'd understood. In his experience, Moorcondians spoke a universal language. Historians believed that all people had sprung from the same place and had spread out as the population grew. Perhaps here, in this unchartered part of the world, a different tongue had developed. No matter... Actions always spoke more eloquently of one's intent. Dismounting, he uncoiled the length of rope tied to his saddle and unfurled it.

"Take hold of this, and I'll pull you out." So saying, he tossed the end toward the boy, careful not to smack him in the face, yet making sure it got within grabbing distance.

The boy didn't take hold of the rope immediately. He kept his gaze on Geoff for a few seconds before slowly taking the end, wrapping it around one small hand and grabbing it with the other. His exhaustion was obvious, leading Geoff to wonder how long he'd been stuck. For sure, the scavengers had sensed an imminent meal. As soon as he was certain the boy had a good grip, Geoff slowly pulled. There was more resistance than he'd expected. They'd run into this sucking sand early in their journey. It was a danger in that it trapped one but was easily dealt with if one had a companion and something to use as leverage to drag the victim out. This particular patch appeared small but held on to the boy with greater tenacity. And with the oblivious horse having neither opposable thumbs nor anything to toss at its master even if it did, this young man had been at great risk.

Why is he alone?

Geoff trusted that his men would be scouting the area for others. Surely there was some kind of civilization nearby and someone would miss this boy eventually. He could only hope that they were inclined to be friendly—or at least grateful for his help in this matter if they came upon them now. None of that was more than a fleeting thought. His concentration remained on the boy's gaze, trying to be reassuring with his expression alone, while he carefully pulled him out of the sand. He tried not to pay too much attention to the fact that the boy was exquisite, with slashing cheekbones, long lashes and plump lips. He ignored as well the bare chest, draped by a beaded vest, and the fact that once the boy was fully out of the sand, he wore only a short, tan leather kilt that left his slender legs exposed. His feet were bare.

When the boy was in reach, he held out a hand. With only a brief hesitation, the boy clasped it and let Geoff tug him to a stand on firmer ground. Fine bits of wet sand clung to his otherwise-smooth skin. Geoff had to resist the temptation to wipe it off. His palms fairly itched with the desire to touch. His dick, which had been lethargic during the trip, found new energy. He'd never wanted anyone more in his life than he did this stranger. Not that his interest was going anywhere… The last thing the boy needed was to think his savoir was only after sex as the price for help.

It didn't matter anyway what Geoff wanted. The boy stood with glazed eyes, panting and swaying. Then he keeled over, right into Geoff's waiting arms.

* * * *

Mica woke to a cool night breeze. Not that he was cold, lying as he was under a light blanket of unfamiliar weave. With a sudden clarity, he remembered what had happened — his stupidly missing the quicksand before he'd sunk too far to escape on his own. He'd been so focused on a flock of birds that he'd forgotten to look where he was going. In one unguarded moment, he'd proven his mother right that he spent too much time with his head in the clouds instead of focusing on where he was going. The hot sun had taunted him with death, and he'd begun to truly fear he would die before anyone realized he was missing, until a stranger had come to his rescue — a fierce-looking warrior of an unknown people. In the brief moment before he'd fainted, Mica'd had a chance to appreciate the raw, masculine power in front of him.

He could hear the man now, along with others, their deep voices murmuring around him. He kept his eyes closed, afraid of what new predicament he'd found himself in and worried that his people would walk into danger while out looking for him. Then footsteps approached and his heartbeat sped up. He could feel the presence of something big and warm and smelling of leather and horse.

"You're awake, I believe."

Mica forced himself to open his eyes and face whoever this man was. He blinked in surprise more than in an effort to clear his vision. The impact of seeing him again was no less strong this second time around. It was the green eyes he noticed first, his fear replaced by surprise and curiosity. He'd never met anyone with this man's coloring before. His square face was golden and handsome. His hair was light and cropped very close to his head. And he was dressed far too much for the desert, although given the paleness of his skin, that was probably a good barrier from the sun. He was clearly a warrior of his people, yet his expression was kind.

"Have some water," the man said before Mica could form any words.

His thirst was great, as he would have expected given how long the sun had beaten down on him. When he tried to sit up, however, weakness had him flopping back down. Except the man shot out an arm to cradle Mica's shoulders. He shuddered at the touch, then melted into it, grateful for the strength. The man held a water bag to his mouth, and he drank greedily until he felt slaked. The man seemed to understand that he needed to lie down again, gently lowering him back onto the thin pallet where he lay.

"I thank you," he managed to say, his raspy voice reminding him he'd been trapped in the quicksand for more than a day.

The stranger grinned. "I'm glad to see you awake, finally. This is the first time since you fainted that you've managed to drink voluntarily. We've had to pour the water into you before."

Mica's tired brain had trouble keeping up with the man's strange cadence, but the words made sense, and he caught up pretty quickly. "It was for how long, my fainting?"

The man scrunched up his face, obviously also getting used to Mica's form of speech. "One night. It's nearly dawn now."

The answer relieved him. It hadn't been more than three days since he'd left home. Some more water, food and rest, and he'd be ready to ride back on his own. "Trouble you for food, may I?"

"Of course." The man gestured to someone else. A man not much older than Mica came trotting up. "Cecil, your patient is awake and asking for food. What do you think would settle best on his stomach?"

The man frowned. "Some broth with a bit of hard tack soaked in it. If he handles that well, we can move on to dried meat."

"Excellent. Go fetch it, please." The older stranger turned his attention back to Mica. Something about his gaze was intimidating — in a good way. "Cecil may be young but he's a well-trained medic." He paused. "I suppose you are curious as to who we are."

Mica nodded, more keen to learn about these strangers now that death was no longer a concern.

The man put his hand on his own chest. "I am Sir Geoffrey Arbuthnott of Moorcondia. Geoff, if you like."

That was a very long name, impressively so. This man was someone of importance, he was sure. Certainly he commanded those around him. Mica gestured toward himself. "Mica, I am." There was nothing more to give about himself, other than a description of the People and where he came from, and that would give away their location. He couldn't take that chance. This man might seem kind now, but he could be here intent on raiding.

The stranger—Geoff—inclined his head. "I'm pleased to meet you, Mica, and let me assure you we mean you no harm. We are explorers for our king and intend merely to travel across this desert to see what is here and beyond. Our journey is about curiosity, not warfare."

Mica let all those words swirl around in his head before replying. "A chief, you have?"

"Yes, although we call him a king."

"The strongest, he is?" It was hard to believe that Geoff wasn't the chief of his people. Mica had never seen a man so big.

Geoff chuckled. "Not exactly. But he does rule us, and he wants to know what this part of the world looks like. I and these others are going to spend a long time traveling. We mean no harm to anyone."

Perhaps it was foolish to take those words at face value. Somehow Mica did. "Believe you, I do."

There was no chance for further talk as Cecil returned with a small wooden bowl. "Ah, many thanks.

I'll see to our guest." Geoff took the bowl and turned to Mica. "Do you need help sitting up?"

Mica thought he could manage on his own yet nodded instead. "Please."

Once again, his rescuer wrapped that big, strong arm around his shoulders and lifted him to a sitting position. Mica reveled in the feel of it. No man, other than his father, had ever touched him so, and no one had ever made him feel this funny warmth deep in his belly. His cock tingled with warning. He pressed one hand down on his lap to keep it under control while he tried to take the bowl with the other. Geoff kept hold of it, though, guiding it to his lips. It was caretaking in a way that was both reminiscent of his mother's coddling when he'd been young and also completely different. Perverse as it might be, he was glad to have landed in trouble. If he hadn't, this man might have passed by without a glimpse.

Not that his attraction was going to amount to anything. As he sipped at his broth, he focused on every detail of the experience—the feel of Geoff's strength, the scent of him, the strange sound of his voice and the excitement it incited in his blood. He would make the most of his time with these strangers, and when he returned home, he would keep the knowledge to himself. Unless Geoff was lying about his intent, Mica dared not tell his chief about their lands being trespassed upon. The People had fought hard to claim their place in the world, and warring tribes were always a worry. He knew the chief wouldn't allow Geoff and his men to simply go on their way. The world was a harsh place, and only the strong and ruthless survived.

When he'd had his fill, he lay back down, comfortable but not sleepy. "Of your tribe, tell me you will?"

Geoff sat cross-legged beside him. "Certainly. Will you also tell me about yours?"

Mica lowered his eyes, disappointed. "Cannot."

There were a few moments of silence. "Ah well, fair enough. I don't want you to get in trouble or worry about my intent. I am happy to tell you about my country, though."

It was like being a child again, lying on his pallet, listening to a fun tale. Geoff talked about great stone dwellings that stood on their own, surrounded by lush trees and shrubbery with many flowers. People rode horses but also in large carts, and they clothed themselves in many layers. It was cold in his country during one season with something called 'snow' that seemed too fantastical to be real. Geoff explained more what they were doing and the role of the older man who was more the size of Mica's people with a pot belly and hair only on the sides of his head. This man was making drawings of everything he saw to take back one day to show their king. It was an amazing story and one that lulled him back to sleep before he was ready.

Still, he wasn't afraid. Against all reason, he was sure he was safe with Sir Geoffrey Arbuthnott—a strange man with a long name and the kindness to save the life of someone and ask nothing in return.

* * * *

Mica patted the side of Windmaker's neck, happy to see that she'd been cared for as much as he had. The sun had climbed well into the sky. He had recovered from his ordeal and his provisions were just as he'd left them in his pack, now strapped across his back. His knife was once more belted across his waist. Geoff and his men had taken nothing from him, even as they'd given him back his life. All those warnings from the elders about the danger of others had proven to be untrue with respect to these Moorcondians. It gave him hope that someday the People would not live in isolation. That day had not yet come, however, and he needed to warn Geoff to stay well away from the warriors that roamed the perimeter of the Peoples' land.

He turned to look for Geoff to bid him a reluctant farewell and was surprised to find the man already upon him. He and his men were packed to also leave the oasis.

"Do you have everything you need, Mica?"

Suddenly shy now that he wasn't an invalid, Mica dropped his gaze. "Yes."

"Good. Thanks to this oasis, we do as well. I hope there are more along the way."

Mica nodded. "Find them, you will."

"I'm glad to hear it. Ah," Geoff stepped closer. "I have enjoyed our time together, even though it was based on your difficulties."

Mica lifted his gaze. "Like it as well, I did."

The man's gaze changed. It took on an intense, heated look. "Will you permit me to say good-bye in the way of my people when we part from someone… whose company we like?"

With the man's gaze now focused on Mica's lips, he thought he knew what was coming. The thought of it thrilled him and closed up his throat. He could only nod.

Geoff moved slowly, lowering his mouth to Mica's. There was plenty of time to evade the kiss. That was the last thing he wanted, and when they touched, he closed his eyes and had to bite back a moan. It was over far too quickly. When Geoff pulled away, Mica had to resist the urge to lunge at him.

Geoff chuckled. "That was unkind of me, to us both. It was like giving a thirsty man only a drop of water. I wish we had more time, Mica."

He took in a deep breath, savoring his name on the man's tongue. Then he forced his eyes open and himself to accept reality. This was a brief encounter, nothing more. He would live with the memory and already knew that no man could ever match his desire for Geoff.

Grabbing Windmaker's mane, he vaulted onto her back. There was one last thing he could do for this man who would never be anything more than his fantasy lover. Pointing toward the Peoples' village, he said, "That way, you do not go. Understand?" He peered at the man, willing him to do so without further explanation. It was a risk, but one he felt confident in taking.

Geoff stared at a distance with a stern expression. Then, he smiled at Mica. "Yes, I will heed your warning. I don't want trouble for anyone — you, least of all." He stepped back. "Safe travels, Mica. And stay away from quicksand."

Mica allowed himself one last, long look at the man who'd saved his life while leaving him wanting, before kicking his horse to a gallop. The sooner he returned home, the sooner he could find somewhere private to relive his fantasy.

About the Author

Samantha Cayto is a Boston-area native who practices as a business lawyer by day while writing erotic romance at night—the steamier the better. She likes to push the envelope when it comes to writing about passion and is delighted other women agree that guy-on-guy sex is the hottest ever.

She lives a typical suburban life with her husband, three kids and four dogs. Her children don't understand why they can't read what she writes, but her husband is always willing to lend her a hand—and anything else—when she needs to choreograph a scene.

Samantha loves to hear from readers. You can find her contact information, website details and author profile page at https://www.firstforromance.com/

Sign up for our newsletter and find out about all our romance book releases, eBook sales and promotions, sneak peeks and FREE romance books!

www.ingramcontent.com/pod-product-compliance
Lightning Source LLC
Chambersburg PA
CBHW050533260626
47157CB00004B/1588